She's Not My Friend

PAULINE MCGOWAN

ISBN: 9798750613601

Other books by this author:

TIZER, COMICS AND CRISPS

INSPECTOR ORANGE
IN THE UNDERBUILD WITH A BLUNT
SPOON

THE FRYING PAN IN THE NIGHT
(featuring the awful Inspector Orange)

THE COPY THIEF
(featuring the annoying Inspector Orange)

DON'T MIX THE DEAD

THE SOAPSTAR MURDERS

PICKING OFF THE PETALS

TROUBLE ON DORSET DRIVE

SOMETHING VERY NASTY IN MY BOOT!

FIFTEEN MINUTES OF SHAME

JUST A WINK AND A SMILE

LONDON TO MILAN

A STAB IN THE BACK

UNEXPECTED ITEM IN
THE HUSBAND'S LUGGAGE

THE SHORE

PROLOGUE

Everyone knew Caroline. She made sure of that. She used to boast she had as many enemies as friends. A lot of us would have argued with that statement. More friends than enemies? Really? Caroline didn't really care if she had friends or enemies as long as she could make use of them, and that she was the centre of attention, good or bad. That's what she revelled in: attention.

Now she was back.

But who was on her revised list of suffering?

CHAPTER ONE

Abigail is in the middle of ridding her hair from the tell-tale signs of grey which have started to appear recently. She hates the process not only because it's messy, smelly and time-consuming but also because it's a reminder she is getting older. She is half-way through the process when her mobile rings.

'I'm busy,' she tells it 'Go away.'

Curiosity pushes her into glancing over to see who is calling. She doesn't recognize the number and decides it has to be another irritating scam or hard sell and metaphorically pats herself on the back that she didn't fall for it.

The next caller is her friend Alexandra. She's on FaceTime.

Abigail is sitting on the floor, her legs straddling the now half-full container of dye-mix. She hesitates and then reluctantly swipes the phone open with her gloved hand.

'It's me. I can't see you, Abby. You there? Talk to me sweetie. It's important.'

With her voice showing irritation, she shouts, 'Yeah I know it's you. Your name came up on the phone otherwise I wouldn't have picked up. I'm right in the middle of something.'

'I still can't see you love, only what looks like a rather large chunk of cellulite.'

Abby grabs the phone glaring at her friend's perfect features with negligible covering of make-up and snaps, 'Sometimes I wonder why I call you a friend or indeed keep you as a friend. Reasons one-to-ten please, best first.'

Ignoring the last remark, Zandra says in astonishment, 'Goodness, are you dyeing your hair *yourself?* Poppet, don't you think it's about time you got some professional help?'

'Alexandra—'

'Zandra, please. You know I hate being called Alexandra. It reminds me of boarding school and those awful cold showers. I'm shivering just thinking about it.'

'Fine, *Zandra!* Why are you calling me? Is it only to insult me or do you actually want something?'

Zandra takes an inward breath and says sarcastically, 'Oh, touché! Nice barb but actually I have to confess my mind is somewhat in turmoil due to my obviously mis-placed loyalty in ringing you first with what you might consider unwelcome news.'

Abby decides to continue with her hair rejuvenation propping up the mobile inside one of her sneakers, silently wishing Zandra could smell the ambience of her foot odour as some kind of penance for her insults. Sighing she panders to her friend's usual over-reaction to life in general. 'OK, tell me. What's happened now? Fortnum and Mason not delivered today? Your live lobster walked out of the fridge? Or, there was nothing left in your size at Harvey Nicks? Or is it that you've caught toenail fungus?'

Zandra screams down the phone, 'Toenail fungus? How *dare* you suggest such a thing!' Then she asks, 'What the hell *is* toenail fungus— is it contagious?'

Finding it hard to keep a straight-face, Abby replies, 'Terribly. Before you share a bed with a man you should *always* check his feet first. You never know what those socks are hiding.' Abby giggles slightly imagining Zandra's expression.

'OMG! Frankly I'm going off this whole idea of Tinder dating. If it's not the embarrassingly awkward moment when the waiter informs you that your *gentleman friend* has left the restaurant without paying, it's the terrifying DTS fear and all its disgusting consequences. And now I have to worry about toe fungus, whatever that is.'

Abigail laughs, 'STD, you nutter, not DTS. And it's toe*nail* fungus, the emphasis is on the toes.'

'Sounds terrifying. Is it terminal?'

Abigail's face creases into the broadest smile, 'No course not and to be truthful, you have so much nail varnish plastered on your toes by your manicurist, I'm amazed your shoes fit you anymore. Look forget I said anything. I'm sure you don't have it. Sorry. I shouldn't wind you up.'

Zandra smarting at being called nutty together with being corrected about STD decides to exact her own correction. 'Not manicurist Abby, it's called a *nail technician.* And as for being wound up, you're right, you shouldn't do that, especially as I rang simply to warn you of possible impending doom heading your way. Or did you forget my reason for ringing already? Oh, and while we're in the process of putting things right, I would like to point out that I'm quite hurt about your other remarks. FYI, I ceased trading with Fortnum's years ago, plus, Harvey Nicks *never* runs out of my size— they wouldn't dare. As for the insinuation about the lobster—'

Abigail laughing at her friend, says, 'OK, OK, stop with the reprimand. I get it. I'm suitably chastened. You have my sincerest apologies. Well, go on then break it to me gently what this world-shattering news is that I need to know?' Abigail has learnt never to be phased by Zandra's weekly melodramas.

'She's back.'

'What? I can't hear you. Speak up the internet dropped.'

Zandra hisses, 'Can't shout. It's tricky. I said, *she's back.*'

'Who's back?' Satisfied that her hirsute remedial task is now as good as she can manage, Abigail makes herself visible and waves at Zandra.

A smiling Zandra waves back. Her expression unexpectedly changes to one of admiration. 'Goodness me Abby, I *am* quite astonished. From here it looks like you've done quite a reasonable job on the retouching. Well, *mostly* anyway from what I can see. My compliments to you. It's practically as if you've gone to a bona fide hair salon. Although not *quite* as adept as Pierre. He's such a darling you should try him some time.'

'Yeah, maybe when I win the lottery.'

'By the way about your cellulite—'

Abigail looks as if she is about to explode. As calmly as she can muster, she snaps, 'You have precisely ten seconds before I put the phone down. Ten, nine, eight—'

'All right, maybe that was a little insensitive.'

'Insensitive you call it? Honestly for two pins I'd— oh never mind. Shall we instead return to the subject of your phone call? Before one of us dies of old age or boredom, put me out of my misery. Who's back?' She pauses. 'Oh, crikey don't tell me it's not your ex-mother-in-law? You poor thing I feel for you. Should I get her effigy out now, ready for the pin-sticking?' she adds grinning.

'No-o-o-o, God, don't, please, *that* would be a cross I simply couldn't bear. Although for you this is possibly as bad, or maybe worse, and then again—'

'Zandra!'

Zandra's face wrinkles. 'Did you really make an effigy? I thought you were only joking because if the old bat finds out—?'

'Zandra please! I'm going to have to disappear and get all this shit off my head in a minute before my hair falls out. Get to the point. Quickly.'

'Sorry, sorry— imagination is on steroids since— since—' and then her voice gets softer. Her head swivels around as if she's checking that no-one's listening. She whispers, 'It's Caroline.'

Irritated Abigail says, 'I can't hear you. I can only see your lips moving. You'll have to speak up, it's quite noisy this end. Our mental neighbours next door are deconstructing their property again. I'm sick of it. I'm convinced if they do much more the whole place will cave in.' As she says the words, she tries to push bad thoughts about them from her mind.

Zandra mouths the words in repeat until suddenly Abigail registers what she is trying to tell her.

'Caroline is back?'

Zandra nods.

Abigail is swearing, profusely, struggling not to drop the phone into the spent hair dye tub, her eyes widening the more she considers the awful revelation. 'You are kidding me, right? Caroline has come back? Here? After all this time? What did we do to deserve that? I don't believe it.' Her lips retract behind her teeth as she bites into them. She shrugs her shoulders and near spits. 'Oh, so what? Couldn't care less if she's here or Outer Mongolia. She doesn't exist as far as I'm concerned. I don't want anything to do with her. A piece of advice, Zandra: if I were you, I'd immediately do one of your famous long-winded texts and tell the gang to lay low.' She pauses a minute and then asks, 'Wait, how do you know this? Who told you?' Then horror-stricken, she twigs. 'Oh my God, she's already been in touch, hasn't she? You've spoken to her already, haven't you? Please tell me you haven't.'

Zandra ignores the insult about her *long-winded* texts. Launching a defence about that isn't going to help the situation. There is an awkward silence as Zandra looks around again nervously. She is stumbling for words until she says quite loudly, 'Isn't it time you rinsed off Abigail? Don't leave it on too long, that's what happened to a good friend of mine who—'

Abigail's eyes narrow, her mind filling with suspicion as each second passes. She waves the comment away with her gloved hand. 'Never mind about my hair, Alexandra. Who exactly told you she was coming back here?'

She whispers again, 'Not coming back *exactly*—she *is* back. I, um, we had lunch yesterday.'

Zandra pulls the phone away from here ear as Abigail screams down the phone, 'You had *lunch* with her yesterday? After everything she did to you, let alone what she's done to the rest of us. You *ate* with her? Like a normal person? Oh my God! What did you talk about? Oh no, let me guess. First of all, you filled her in with all the goss, didn't you? You are such an easy target. I suppose she got out of you that Baz and I have split up? No answer? Thought not, you beast. Shit Alexandra, you are hopeless, entirely hopeless. Where was all the *I'm done with her, I've given her a final warning, I've blocked her on my phone, I've*, oh I don't know? Basically, you assured me on your favourite dog's grave that you'd told her to *do one*. Now you're telling me you've had *lunch* with her. *Lunch!* Who lunches with the enemy? I tell you who—a lily-livered moron, that's who.'

Again, she decides against defending herself in the face of the venom pouring from Abigail's mouth. She meekly offers instead, 'Yes, awkward, isn't it?'

'Awkward, awkward, you call it awkward? I call it insane, downright stupid, completely off the wall nuts! Masochistic even. Sadistic when you include us, your so-called friends. Why did you break the pact? She's a walking trouble-making piece of shit—'

'That's a bit harsh Abigail.'

'Harsh! Harsh! Is that strong enough a word? I don't think so? I can be even more *harsh* if you want? I can be the epitome of harsh. I can make the word harsh feel like the down on goose's arse. She should be locked up for all the stuff she's done. She would be in more unenlightened times, possibly even stoned to death. There's a thought that appeals to me.' Then seeing Zandra's terrified expression, Abigail backtracks, 'OK, OK, maybe that's a bit too far, even for her, but honestly you need to cut that woman loose straight away. Get shot of her because she blights all of our—'

Suddenly the screen changes. A different face appears, looming large, head on one side, teeth so white that for a moment Abigail has to blink at their luminosity.

'Oh hi, Abigail, I wondered who Alexandra was talking to? Oh, my word. What's that on your head? Don't tell me you're having to *dye* your hair already? You're a couple of months older than me, aren't you? I remember now. How *are* you honey? Me? I'm thrilled to be back home, at long last. It's been hell. I tell you, if it wasn't for Alexandra here, I don't know what I would have done. She's such a star. A true friend.'

Abigail's face is suddenly drained of colour. She's not embarrassed by her half-cooked hair or the fact that Caroline had more than likely Caroline heard every condemnatory word uttered. She's just realised there's no way to escape this bitch. It's obvious who Alexandra's new house guest is.

But for how long?
And   why?

CHAPTER TWO

Abigail glances upwards at the impending storm overhead. She turns on her windscreen wipers as a few large spots of rain splatter her vision. A sudden flash of lightning brightens the darkening sky. She mutters to herself, 'Great, that's all I need, getting stuck in a thunderstorm.'

She asks herself why she is doing this? Why is she putting herself into Caroline's firing line of humiliation? Although she had a feeble attempt earlier at removing herself the day before.

Feigning a heavy cold by coughing intermittently she had said hoarsely, 'Not feeling so good Zandra.' Cough. Cough. 'I'm positive I'm coming down with something horrible.' Cough. Cough. 'Probably best I don't turn up and infect you all with something nasty.' Like Caroline, Abigail thinks.

Zandra rounded on her instantly. 'Oh no you don't, you're not backing out now you coward. I know when you're putting it on. Apart from your pathetic lacklustre excuse that *you're not feeling well,* surely you could have come up with something a bit more believable. Honestly you criticise me for a lack of imagination? Besides, I keep telling you, it's like some kind of miracle. The hand of God—'

'That's football. The world Cup. Maradona. Absolutely nothing to do with calculating Caroline.'

'Don't interrupt Abigail; it's very rude. As the saying goes, *manners maketh the man.*'

Interrupting again, Abigail demands, 'So what maketh the woman then? Putting up with bitchy women? Tolerating scumbags? Being bamboozled by—'

'Stop. Enough. Please before you say something you'll regret.'

'Point one. You just interrupted me. Point two, I will never, ever regret anything bad I say about Caroline. There are no words strong enough to describe the abject animosity I feel for that *person* on planet Earth.'

Zandra sighs, 'I wish you would unblock your prejudice against her. Seriously, she's transformed herself—'

'Oh, what like a born-again human being?'

Abigail can hear the frustration in Zandra's voice as she continues, 'Caroline's a different person now, kind, considerate, generous. What's more she's desperate to make amends with you. She doesn't talk of much else. You've got to give her a chance to rectify things. She wants to explain what she was going through at the time. Why she did what she did.'

Abigail can hardly disguise the contempt in her voice. 'What *she* was going through at the time? Like what? Having a good time with everybody's boyfriends in bed? My God, it must have been hell for her. One wonders how she got through it all. Zandra, listen to yourself. I can't believe you've swallowed all her crap about her miraculous turnaround from bitch to nun. Was there a sudden bolt of lightning from the sky? Or did she find her true self in a Tibetan monastery? You are so gullible. And you really think I'm going to give her a chance to rectify things with me? How would that work? Bit late in the day, seeing how she was the person who pushed the eject button down hard on our wedding day. Honestly and truthfully Zandra, would you be so generous as to forgive her if the boot was on the other foot?'

'Shoe, poppet, the term is shoe, even though I must say boots are obviously more in vogue this season. I bought a simply darling pair of ankle boots online from—'

'Yeah, whatever, you can show me when I get there alongside all the other bargains you've *snatched* that collectively total more than most people earn in a year.'

Zandra snorts in derision but at the same time she knows she has Abigail on the back foot, or boot, or shoe, or whatever now. Zandra wants her there, needs her there even if only for support. At the back of Zandra's mind there is a tiny niggling doubt that maybe Caroline is acting out a part. She may *not* have changed at all. She's positive that with Abigail's sixth sense all will become clear. As for the other three friends, particularly Victoria, who has only recently come out of her Habitat closet, she's not convinced they'll believe Caroline has changed either. Zandra questions her own ability to see through people's deception; it's been one of her failings. She knows she's a soft touch.

Therefore, Abigail decides there is no way out. She has to go. She spends ages choosing and discarding outfits from her wardrobe until her daughter, curious as to why she is not wearing her usual jeans, top and ubiquitous jacket, demands to know why the fuss?

'A person from the past will be there.'

'A *person* from the past? Wow! Mummy's being a bit mysterious,' scoffs Hannah, her fifteen-year-old. Then waving her hands around her eyes looking wild and scared she follows through with a ghostly *ooh-ooh-aah-aah-ooh-aah* noise, adding softly, 'Be careful not to turn your back Mum, you never know who is behind you.' More oohs and aahs until she collapses into a fit of giggles at her own silliness.

'Oh, very funny, very droll. But you've got one thing right, I certainly won't be turning my back on her.I used to be friends with that *person*. She was my best friend until she—'

'Until she what? Stole your boyfriend?' she interrupts, arms folded, eyebrows raised. 'So what's new? That's the norm, isn't it? Always has been. Best friend steals boyfriend? Happens all the time especially on social media. And definitely on Love Island.'

Abigail mutters under her breath, '*Love Island.*'

Hannah suddenly realises she's hit a nerve, 'Oh Mum I'm sorry. Please don't look so sad. I didn't mean to upset you. So, it still hurts then, does it? Who is this woman, this boyfriend-stealing person? Tell me and I'll sort her out once and for all.'

Abigail smiles at her daughter, 'That's sweet of you but I don't think so. Her name's Caroline, Caroline

Smith. At least it used to be Smith when we were at school together. Goodness knows what it is now. She's been married and divorced at least twice that I know of.' Abigail dismisses the subject as if it's now of no consequence, 'You've never met her thank goodness. It was long before you were born, aeons ago.'

'Even so, it's so obvious you're not over it,' she says, 'and actually you're wrong. I think I do know *exactly* who you're talking about. She's the person in the photo you've folded out of sight in the frame on the desk, isn't she?'

Abigail is astonished, 'How do you know about that?'

Defensively she blusters, 'I wasn't snooping if that's what you're thinking before you have a go at me. I saw Dad looking at it one day and asked him who it was. He went completely weird about it. I remember at the time wondering why, seeing as he said she was *your* friend. I was going to ask you but then it slipped my mind. Is it because you all used to hang out together? Is that how he knows her?'

Abigail takes a deep breath. Does she tell her daughter about Baz's first dalliance after their marriage? The day of their marriage even? How she found Caroline, her maid of honour, and Baz exploring each other's bodies? How both pretended they were so drunk they didn't know what they were doing? That initial betrayal never left Abigail all throughout their marriage and reared its ugly head like the proverbial sea-monster anytime there was a spat between them. She couldn't help it. And he, her husband, would accuse her of never letting that *error of judgement* go, insisting it was her lack of trust in him which made him continue in his philandering ways, allegedly pushed into them by her constant jealous questioning. How easy it is to find an excuse for your own bad behaviour and blame it on someone else.

'It's a long sad story. Let's simply say she was a good friend until she wasn't and leave it at that.'

'But Dad—'

'But Dad nothing.'

Hannah senses maybe it isn't such a good idea to push the interrogation. She starts sifting through the clothes on the bed. The teenager has recently transformed into a young fashionista. The previous week found her upstairs in the attic frantically rummaging around in a suitcase full of Abigail's outmoded clothes, shrieking with delight when she exclaimed, 'Oh my God, this is *so in* right now, can I have it? Do you mind?'

Now while Abigail sits dejectedly cross-legged on the floor debating what to wear, Hannah has decided to take over. She studies the discarded skirts, blouses, jumpers, suits, wrinkling her nose at Abigail's choices and announces pompously, emulating a sniffy saleswoman from a posh-over-the-top-priced store, 'I'm sure we can find you the perfect thing to wear; after all, mother, *I am* the one that reads all the fashion magazines, not you.'

'Yeah, but I pay for them.' Abigail involuntarily smiles. Her daughter is finally growing up and taking charge. Boy is she is loving every minute of it. Good for her, thinks Abigail. Long may it last.

Occasionally the teenager puts some of the outfits against herself, admiring the image in the mirror or other times dropping them back on the bed as if they are covered in pigeon excreta. At the bottom of the pile is a red dress. 'Wow, did you actually buy *this*? It's *so* expensive,' she says, her eyes popping at the price tag, her mind calculating that her mother might have a good deal more money than she had previously thought.

'Yes of course I bought it. And you can get that look out of your eyes. Stop wondering how I could afford it. There was an online reduction of 70% and then I found another 20% discount code. I'm not made of money. Can't wear it anyway. It was a stupid and reckless buy. One size too small.'

'What do you mean? Come on let's see you in it. I'm sure we can sort something out.'

There she was again, the bossy, sniffy saleswoman.

Abigail is bullied into trying it. Huffing and puffing, she struggles to pull the dress down over her various bulges. 'See,' she says sadly, 'I told you it was far too small.' Even so she stares at herself in the mirror, twisting and turning, holding in her breath and straightening her back. Pulling a face she asks plaintively, 'Do you think I could get away with it?'

Her daughter's reply is not encouraging. She nods, 'I'm not so sure. You are right. It is far too small. It's especially tight over your rear end; actually makes it look bigger than it really is.'

Abigail wants to scream, 'Stop right there. Enough with the criticism.' But she holds back. Bonding with Hannah is very rare these days.

Hannah though is in full *helpful* mode. 'Mum if you're asking me to be truly honest, I think you actually look positively uncomfortable in it.' Before Abigail has a chance to, Hannah shouts, 'Don't do that! Don't sit down. Seriously all the seams will pop and we'll have a nightmare getting it off you.' It crosses Hannah's mind she may have been just a little too honest with her opinions, so she backtracks, 'At least, that's what I think. But I'm just a kid, what do I know?'

'Thanks.' Abigail is wondering if she should give some advice about Hannah's bluntness. It's a good way to lose friends.

Her expression must have given her away because Hannah says, 'You don't have to give me a dirty look, you did ask me what I thought. Seeing as you did ask my opinion may I say you're trying too hard? If I was the *person, this Caroline,* whom we both now obviously despise, I'd look at you in that dress and feel pretty smug that you'd gone to all the bother of impressing me.'

Hannah dives into the wardrobe looking through the remainder of the clothes hanging and pulls out a patchwork waistcoat still with its labels attached. 'See now this would work with everything, great with jeans, trousers, or even a skirt. This would be my choice.'

Abigail scrunches up her face and says dismissively, 'No, better not.'

'What do you mean "better not"? Oh God, Mum, don't tell me you nicked it? Is that why all the labels are still on it?' She looks animated and says, 'Wow, are you a shoplifter all of a sudden because if you are there's this blouse I saw in—'

Horrified, Abigail says vehemently, 'No I am not a shoplifter. What the hell's the matter with you? Just because your father's left me doesn't mean to say I'm off the wall nuts.'

Having performed a rerun of all the clothes piled on the bed and come to exactly the same conclusion as she had done half an hour before, Abigail begrudgingly bends to her daughter's suggestion and teams the waistcoat with a pair of cream trousers and a plain cream silk blouse.

'There,' says Hannah in her expanding patronising tone, smoothing down the waistcoat at the back, running her finger down the creases of the trousers in the front in true shop-assistant style. She says, 'See, that's *much* better. Definitely you. Not too showy or too young. Ladies of your age have to be careful not to look mutton-dressed-as-spring-lamb. I see it all the time in the magazines— abandoned women desperate to recapture their lost youth in an attempt to attract new lovers.' Abigail stares at her, not quite knowing what to say to her teenager with her braced teeth and disguised acne. Her totally undiplomatic daughter.

Hannah cups her elbow with one hand, rubbing her chin with the other, head on one side, and says, 'I have to admit Mum, Dad dumping you has done wonders for your figure. You look pretty sensational.'

A compliment? Abigail is not sure but decides to take it. She needs it these days. It gives her a little more confidence as she steps into her car slightly confused but hopefully looking reasonably good. But as she drives through the suburban roads which eventually roll out into the countryside where Zandra's Georgian mansion is situated, Abigail's confidence in her outfit, her straightened hair, her general demeanour starts to slide down into the mire once more. After all, what did her teenage daughter, hardly a woman of the world and just a kid, know about fashion and trying to create an aura of natural sophistication and *who-gives-a-damn?*

The rain is getting heavier now and the windscreen wipers are on full. Abigail is finding it difficult to drive. Mindful of the need to suddenly brake, she is hanging back from the car in front even though the driver behind her is finding this irritating. She waves at him to back off. This gesture seems to annoy him even more and all she can see in her rear-view mirror is his headlights blinding her. She curses Zandra for pushing her into doing something her whole instinct told her was doomed to failure. Now to crown it all she is the potential victim of road rage in a thunderstorm.

The road bends and the impatient road-hog behind suddenly pulls out causing her and the unsuspecting driver in front to swerve. Somehow there is no collision but the shot of adrenalin to the heart is massive. Strangely it helps.

She yells out, 'Sod you Caroline.' She punches the radio on and laughs as the tune playing is, 'I will survive.' She sings at the top of her voice banging the steering wheel at times in tune to the beat.

In her peripheral vision Abigail is aware of the patchwork waistcoat. Like the red dress she had planned to wear, it too has a designer label but also carries another label, one of disillusion, betrayal and finality. That label was the reason Abigail found herself so reticent in choosing it. The unexpected discovery of the beribboned box hidden in the back of her husband's section of the wardrobe was the final nail in their marriage coffin.

When she'd first found it, Abigail had been excited beyond belief. How wonderful to think Baz had bought her a surprise present when there was no birthday or anniversary celebration nearby. It was so out of character. Something he hadn't done in years. Maybe there was hope for them both after all. Particularly as this coincided with his continual absences from home. It seemed there were fewer and fewer occasions when their paths crossed. But as the days wore on and the package hadn't budged an inch from its hidey-hole, Abigail became impatient for it to be handed over to her. What was he waiting for? Was its destiny to be a reward for an extra especially nice Sunday lunch?

One night her mostly no-show husband had rung to say that yet again he was working late at the office and would probably sleep on the couch there. Abigail's curiosity about him and the package had been pushed into overdrive. She lay in the bed tossing and turning wondering exactly what he was doing and with whom? Her insides had been in turmoil. The bed had turned into concrete. Her pillows the same. Her legs were restless, she was hot then cold, hot, cold, uncomfortable and totally wide awake. The hours ticked by. The minutes ticked by. The seconds ticked by. And all the time the box seemed to be calling out for her to discover its contents.

She'd slid out of bed. Nervously checked and rechecked the curtains were drawn tight shut. Desperate not to be discovered in her snooping, she had even gone downstairs to make sure the front door was locked and bolted in case Baz changed his mind, arrived home and caught her red-handed. She'd crept back up the stairs and pulled out the parcel. She stared at it. Rattled it. Poked it. Debated if it was possible the wrapping would come loose accidently on purpose. Finally, she'd given in. The ribbons were a nightmare to undo without damaging them but she'd managed it. She'd carefully pulled off the sticky circular plastic tabs fastening down the lid without making so much as the slightest tear then gingerly she'd opened the box. Whatever secret the box contained it was being cossetted by pure white tissue again fastened by a circular stick-on label. Abigail didn't recognise the brand name. Inside the tissue was the designer patchwork waistcoat and an envelope addressed to someone called Rebecca.

It was as if she had been turned to stone. Or was it jelly? She felt she had no control of her limbs. She was transfixed. Abigail felt as if she was in another dimension. It was almost an out-of-body experience. It wasn't pleasant. There was no triumph in the realisation that all her doubts and fears had been transformed into reality. All those excuses she had made to bolster up her anxieties over his absences were all to no avail. There was no stepping back in time. This was a hard fact which was impossible to ignore. At first, she'd felt unable to breath. Her blood pressure had risen off the scale. The next minute her body was shaking with the shock. She felt icy cold as if her heart was being held tight by an ice monster's hand, its bony fingers digging into her very soul. That heart which until five minutes beforehand had held so much love in it for her husband was now coldly pounding, loudly enough that she thought she was going to have a stroke there and then and die on the spot. Who would find her the next day slumped over the box with the waistcoat? Her daughter Hannah? Or would it be Baz her worthless cheating husband? What would he think? Would he shed a tear? Would he have any regret? Somehow, she didn't think so. Would he be pleased? Would he think smugly, *Well, that saved a bundle of cash on a divorce?'*

With trembling hands, she took the note and punished her tortured mind even more by reading it.

'Darling Rebecca, I saw this and immediately thought of you. Remember Venice and that steamy, glorious night on the canal when we paid the boatman to look away?'

That was it then?

She'd been a mug. She'd been lied to and had swallowed every lie. All the pointers and suspicions recently that Baz was sleeping with someone else which she had chosen to explain away and ignore, well they were all true. Like a lightning bolt from the sky all the jigsaw pieces started to meld together into a horrible life-changing image. She recalled the weekend she and Hannah had spent in Scotland with her grandmother. Baz had been uncontactable. His phone had rung out constantly, his excuse the usual *No signal, love, internet problems, what can you do?* Overwhelmingly, heart-in-mouth, she now realised why. He couldn't be available to make or receive phone calls because the foreign dial-tone would have been a dead giveaway. Besides, he had no need for it while he was having fun with his girlfriend.

At first Abigail's immediate reaction was to ring him there and then, wake him up, wherever he was and scream down the phone at him but it was unlikely he'd answer if his phone was even switched on. She knew she would end up pressing redial over and over and over again, adding to the humiliation.

Instead, she repackaged everything as it was and stuck it back into place. He could keep his low-life secret intact as far as she was concerned. She lay on the bed but there was no way she could fall asleep. She had suspected he had been cheating on her, but now, with proof, her mind had gone nuclear. Images of passion such as she used to enjoy with her husband were replaced by the imagined body of Rebecca. It was an assault to her brain. Was she blonde? Brunette? Redhead? Young? An hour-glass figure with huge breasts? Perfectly rounded bottom and long never-ending legs? Visions of him writhing with this Rebecca woman made her sick to her stomach. Exhausted she finally drifted off only then to experience torturously vivid nightmares where this Rebecca person was naked beneath the fancy gifted waistcoat and her husband.

Her anger suddenly took hold of her. How dare he, how dare he do this to her? How could he have insinuated she was insane with her accusations when all the time her instincts had been bang on. He wasn't just cheating on her but also on his daughter, his beloved Hannah. How could he be so very cruel? She hated him for that, she hated and despised him more than anything or anyone else in the whole of her life. She cried tears of rage alongside tears of hurt and pain. Of betrayal and spent love. And flashes of happier times kept annoyingly hitting her brain. Questions. Why? Why? Why? Had she been such a bad wife, a lover, a friend, that he felt no qualms about having done this to her? Did he have no conscience or guilt in his treacherous cheating body?

Didn't look like it.

At 5 am she said to herself *Sod it, the cow Rebecca can have my worthless husband but she's not getting the Venetian reminder. I'll cut it up or burn it before that happens.*

Having previously undone the package carefully and then even more carefully put it back together, this time she ripped the packaging apart and tore it into tiny pieces. Her rage consuming her. She was about to do the same with the waistcoat but then something stopped her. She googled the brand and was horrified to discover exactly how much he'd spent on it. And therefore, on her! The harlot. The slut. The whore. The husband stealer. The bitch.

She visualised his face when she confronted him with his infidelity. She could hear his protestations, his feeble excuses, see his fake imploring eyes. His stories had always sounded so believable and with foundation that he could turn her suspicions into paranoia. But how could he deny hard fact? A waistcoat! A written note!

Abigail stuffed the note into the front slip pocket of the waistcoat and stuck it on a hanger shoving it into her section of the wardrobe. She was desperate for him to notice it, to see the expression on his face when he realised the game was finally up.

Somehow the following day through grim determination as Abigail applied her make-up, she fixed a smile on her face. She tried to act normally as if it were an ordinary carefree day, dropping off her daughter at school and then onward to work. She'd found it hard to concentrate. She was still nauseous from the sleepless night. She couldn't eat. All the time she was continually thinking ahead to the evening when she would demand an explanation, planning her action, formulating her speeches. Absurdly she had to suffer a longer wait for her unfaithful husband as he didn't arrive back for another two days. When he finally turned up, she was ill-prepared. Words, speeches, actions, all forgotten. As much as she tried, her rehearsed plan of action could not be retrieved from her grief-stricken mind.

Luckily, Hannah was staying overnight with a friend when Abigail walked through the front door to find her husband sitting there with his coat on in the dark drinking coffee and smoking.

'Oh, you're home then,' she'd said, coldly.

'Bit obvious. Yes, I'm home.'

'And smoking! Hmm, what a surprise! Thought you sworn you'd given that up for good?' she'd added, even more icily.

'So did I.' He'd then lit another with the smouldering almost spent cigarette defiantly, taunting her to make another comment and said, 'Circumstances.'

'Circumstances? That's what you call it.'

Abigail's heart was thumping. She had rage but she also had fear, anxiety, terror. The terror of suddenly being alone in the world with Hannah minus support, especially financial support. She was at that point of no return that so many marriages encounter when a confrontation would mean the total collapse and end of the alliance. Once those words, those accusations had been spoken and were out in the ether for all to hear, there was no way back. No time-machine. No replay-button. Many times she'd bitten her tongue, wary of such a finality because of Hannah. But Hannah was now fifteen. Which was worse, her living in a household of lies and deceit *with* her father or in a hopefully more harmonious atmosphere where maybe money would be tight, the house might be sold, but her life might be more honest? It was an almost impossible choice. Did she have the courage to make that decision? Would she allow *circumstances* to drift along so that it wouldn't be her decision but that of her husband's?

With hesitation devouring her, Abigail bit her tongue. Those previous days and nights of anguish choked her, stuck in her throat like an oversized pill that was hard to swallow. She debated with herself if she was doing the right thing. Maybe this was yet another fling which would run its course; had run its course just like all the others. She'd been accused of over-reacting enough times before. Maybe she had driven Baz to these lengths because of her mistrust of him all these years.

Then she spotted the suitcase by the door. She was puzzled at first and then angry. She felt like a fool. He'd come home to pack for probably another jolly jaunt with *Rebecca*. Ugh, how she hated that name. She'd known a couple of Rebecca's in her life. One was at school. Becky. Horrible, nasty, trouble-making Becky. There was the one at work in her first job, Becca. Too posh to make the tea for everyone. And now *her*, the husband thief.

'I'm leaving you.'

Just like that. He'd said it just like that!

'What?' She couldn't have heard him correctly. She must have imagined the words.

'You heard. I'm leaving you. OK?' he'd said.

There was silence. Hanging there between them like a hovering wasp, its venom pointing in both directions.

'Leaving me?' she'd said. 'Yeah, I heard the words. I just don't believe them. *You* are leaving *me?* That's rich, that's so up-your-arse rich! How about I'm throwing you out instead?'

He hadn't looked around, drawing down on the cigarette to take a long hit of nicotine and shrugged, 'Suit yourself. Same difference.' The words had been uttered in a monotone. A throw-away line as if he didn't care. Had never cared. She was incensed.

The avalanche of hurt began slowly and then built at speed. Everything came spilling out, the years of angst, nights of no sleep, the worry of STDs, the betrayal of her and his daughter; it was endless. A veritable tsunami of words she let loose, the dam of torture that had been stored inside her had burst. It should have been a relief, the fact she'd held back, churning the words and thoughts inside her for all those years. Yet it wasn't. It was all out now. All said. No pulling back. No change of heart from either party. The die had been cast. She was empty, hollow, vacant, drained.

What did Baz do?

Nothing.

He sat there listening. Then slowly stubbed out his cigarette. Stood up, pushed her to one side, gently manhandling her shoulders so he could get past. Picked up his suitcase and walked through the front door without a backward glance. He didn't slam the door but pulled it to, so quietly Abigail wasn't convinced he'd even shut it.

Abigail had stood still with silent tears falling down her cheeks thick and fast, her knees trembling, her whole body shaking. She felt weak and unable to stand. She'd slumped to the floor in a heap, almost in a foetal position. Abigail must have stayed like that for a good ten minutes before it hit her that her marriage was definitely over and there was no way back for either of them even if they'd wanted one.

Afterwards she'd wondered why she hadn't even asked him to stay, or for an explanation as to why he was leaving? And who was Rebecca? And how long had this affair been going on? And what was he going to say to Hannah? And what about the house? And the mortgage? And—and—and—and, so many ands, so many things, and now he was gone, with no answers, no explanations, no sign of remorse, or apologies.

Nothing.

Silence.

Coldness.

Disconnected.

Abigail was distraught. So many questions left unanswered. No answers to so many questions. So much hurt, so much pain that when Hannah came home Abigail didn't know what to tell her.

'Fancy a take-out tonight love?' she'd asked, trying to control the tremble in her voice.

'Take-out? What on a Wednesday? Did we win the lottery or something?'

Then Abigail had broken down. Hannah knew immediately. She didn't need any explanation. She was a bright thing. 'Don't worry Mum, we'll manage until Dad sees sense and comes back.'

How could she tell Hannah he wasn't coming back? She knew deep down he never would. Anyway, she didn't want him back. Or did she? Abigail was in a torment of mixed feelings. Before all she could think of was his moodiness and no-shows at school events; his lack of support when she needed it most; his increasing absences. Now, all the memories were good ones, of laughter, fun and stupidity, of times when she believed nothing could end their love for each other and nothing could ever destroy them. But it had.

That was four months ago. Discussions were since directed through solicitors. Hannah had seen her father a couple of times and a couple of times he hadn't shown. But the waistcoat was still here. That hadn't moved out. It symbolised everything about her marriage, hanging there, taunting her. Until Hannah pulled it off the rail and told Abigail to try it on.

It would puzzle Abigail from time to time afterwards why she had let Hannah persuade her into wearing the wretched thing. Most people, she thought, would have had the sense to tear it to shreds or at least give it to a charity shop, or tried to sell it on eBay. But somehow the designer waistcoat was an important symbol. One of defiance. Yes, maybe Rebecca had won her husband form her but then again maybe she hadn't won anything. Maybe they hadn't even been an item and Abigail's assumption had been wrong. Or if they were together, they weren't now. Who knew and who cared? But Abigail, like the song on the radio said, was a survivor and survivors used every weapon they could lay their hands on. The waistcoat in a peculiar way, was the colourful expensive statement Abigail needed to keep that said she didn't care about being deserted by a worthless man.

So, she was trying to wear it proudly. It was original. It was expensive. It was hers, now, because Rebecca could never receive it. It was a small victory and she would use it to fortify herself against the no doubt oncoming onslaught of Caroline and her continuing, unexplained vendetta against Abigail and her friends.

CHAPTER THREE

Abigail glances upwards at the impending storm overhead. She turns on her windscreen wipers as a few large spots of rain splatter her vision. A sudden flash of lightning brightens the darkening sky. She mutters to herself, 'Great, that's all I need, getting stuck in a thunderstorm.'

She asks herself why she is doing this? Why is she putting herself into Caroline's firing line of humiliation? Although she had a feeble attempt earlier at removing herself the day before.

Feigning a heavy cold by coughing intermittently she had said hoarsely, 'Not feeling so good Zandra.' Cough. Cough. 'I'm positive I'm coming down with something horrible.' Cough. Cough. 'Probably best I don't turn up and infect you all with something nasty.' Like Caroline, Abigail thinks.

Zandra rounded on her instantly. 'Oh no you don't, you're not backing out now you coward. I know when you're putting it on. Apart from your pathetic lacklustre excuse that *you're not feeling well,* surely you could have come up with something a bit more believable. Honestly you criticise me for a lack of imagination? Besides, I keep telling you, it's like some kind of miracle. The hand of God—'

'That's football. The world Cup. Maradona. Absolutely nothing to do with calculating Caroline.'

'Don't interrupt Abigail; it's very rude. As the saying goes, *manners maketh the man.'*

Interrupting again, Abigail demands, 'So what maketh the woman then? Putting up with bitchy women? Tolerating scumbags? Being bamboozled by—'

'Stop. Enough. Please before you say something you'll regret.'

'Point one. You just interrupted me. Point two, I will never, ever regret anything bad I say about Caroline. There are no words strong enough to describe the abject animosity I feel for that *person* on planet Earth.'

Zandra sighs, 'I wish you would unblock your prejudice against her. Seriously, she's transformed herself—'

'Oh, what like a born-again human being?'

Abigail can hear the frustration in Zandra's voice as she continues, 'Caroline's a different person now, kind, considerate, generous. What's more she's desperate to make amends with you. She doesn't talk of much else. You've got to give her a chance to rectify things. She wants to explain what she was going through at the time. Why she did what she did.'

Abigail can hardly disguise the contempt in her voice. 'What *she* was going through at the time? Like what? Having a good time with everybody's boyfriends in bed? My God, it must have been hell for her. One wonders how she got through it all. Zandra, listen to yourself. I can't believe you've swallowed all her crap about her miraculous turnaround from bitch to nun. Was there a sudden bolt of lightning from the sky? Or did she find her true self in a Tibetan monastery? You are so gullible. And you really think I'm going to give her a chance to rectify things with me? How would that work? Bit late in the day, seeing how she was the person who pushed the eject button down hard on our wedding day. Honestly and truthfully Zandra, would you be so generous as to forgive her if the boot was on the other foot?'

'Shoe, poppet, the term is shoe, even though I must say boots are obviously more in vogue this season. I bought a simply darling pair of ankle boots online from—'

'Yeah, whatever, you can show me when I get there alongside all the other bargains you've *snatched* that collectively total more than most people earn in a year.'

Zandra snorts in derision but at the same time she knows she has Abigail on the back foot, or boot, or shoe, or whatever now. Zandra wants her there, needs her there even if only for support. At the back of Zandra's mind there is a tiny niggling doubt that maybe Caroline is acting out a part. She may *not* have changed at all. She's positive that with Abigail's sixth sense all will become clear. As for the other three friends, particularly Victoria, who has only recently come out of her Habitat closet, she's not convinced they'll believe Caroline has changed either. Zandra questions her own ability to see through people's deception; it's been one of her failings. She knows she's a soft touch.

Therefore, Abigail decides there is no way out. She has to go. She spends ages choosing and discarding outfits from her wardrobe until her daughter, curious as to why she is not wearing her usual jeans, top and ubiquitous jacket, demands to know why the fuss?

'A person from the past will be there.'

'A *person* from the past? Wow! Mummy's being a bit mysterious,' scoffs Hannah, her fifteen-year-old. Then waving her hands around her eyes looking wild and scared she follows through with a ghostly *ooh-ooh-aah-aah-ooh-aah* noise, adding softly, 'Be careful not to turn your back Mum, you never know who is behind you.' More oohs and aahs until she collapses into a fit of giggles at her own silliness.

'Oh, very funny, very droll. But you've got one thing right, I certainly won't be turning my back on her.I used to be friends with that *person*. She was my best friend until she—'

'Until she what? Stole your boyfriend?' she interrupts, arms folded, eyebrows raised. 'So what's new? That's the norm, isn't it? Always has been. Best friend steals boyfriend? Happens all the time especially on social media. And definitely on Love Island.'

Abigail mutters under her breath, *'Love Island.'*

Hannah suddenly realises she's hit a nerve, 'Oh Mum I'm sorry. Please don't look so sad. I didn't mean to upset you. So, it still hurts then, does it? Who is this woman, this boyfriend-stealing person? Tell me and I'll sort her out once and for all.'

Abigail smiles at her daughter, 'That's sweet of you but I don't think so. Her name's Caroline, Caroline

Smith. At least it used to be Smith when we were at school together. Goodness knows what it is now. She's been married and divorced at least twice that I know of.' Abigail dismisses the subject as if it's now of no consequence, 'You've never met her thank goodness. It was long before you were born, aeons ago.'

'Even so, it's so obvious you're not over it,' she says, 'and actually you're wrong. I think I do know *exactly* who you're talking about. She's the person in the photo you've folded out of sight in the frame on the desk, isn't she?'

Abigail is astonished, 'How do you know about that?'

Defensively she blusters, 'I wasn't snooping if that's what you're thinking before you have a go at me. I saw Dad looking at it one day and asked him who it was. He went completely weird about it. I remember at the time wondering why, seeing as he said she was *your* friend. I was going to ask you but then it slipped my mind. Is it because you all used to hang out together? Is that how he knows her?'

Abigail takes a deep breath. Does she tell her daughter about Baz's first dalliance after their marriage? The day of their marriage even? How she found Caroline, her maid of honour, and Baz exploring each other's bodies? How both pretended they were so drunk they didn't know what they were doing? That initial betrayal never left Abigail all throughout their marriage and reared its ugly head like the proverbial sea-monster anytime there was a spat between them. She couldn't help it. And he, her husband, would accuse her of never letting that *error of judgement* go, insisting it was her lack of trust in him which made him continue in his philandering ways, allegedly pushed into them by her constant jealous questioning. How easy it is to find an excuse for your own bad behaviour and blame it on someone else.

'It's a long sad story. Let's simply say she was a good friend until she wasn't and leave it at that.'

'But Dad—'

'But Dad nothing.'

Hannah senses maybe it isn't such a good idea to push the interrogation. She starts sifting through the clothes on the bed. The teenager has recently transformed into a young fashionista. The previous week found her upstairs in the attic frantically rummaging around in a suitcase full of Abigail's outmoded clothes, shrieking with delight when she exclaimed, 'Oh my God, this is *so in* right now, can I have it? Do you mind?'

Now while Abigail sits dejectedly cross-legged on the floor debating what to wear, Hannah has decided to take over. She studies the discarded skirts, blouses, jumpers, suits, wrinkling her nose at Abigail's choices and announces pompously, emulating a sniffy sales-woman from a posh-over-the-top-priced store, 'I'm sure we can find you the perfect thing to wear; after all, mother, *I am* the one that reads all the fashion magazines, not you.'

'Yeah, but I pay for them.' Abigail involuntarily smiles. Her daughter is finally growing up and taking charge. Boy is she is loving every minute of it. Good for her, thinks Abigail. Long may it last.

Occasionally the teenager puts some of the outfits against herself, admiring the image in the mirror or other times dropping them back on the bed as if they are covered in pigeon excreta. At the bottom of the pile is a red dress. 'Wow, did you actually buy *this*? It's *so* expensive,' she says, her eyes popping at the price tag, her mind calculating that her mother might have a good deal more money than she had previously thought.

'Yes of course I bought it. And you can get that look out of your eyes. Stop wondering how I could afford it. There was an online reduction of 70% and then I found another 20% discount code. I'm not made of money. Can't wear it anyway. It was a stupid and reckless buy. One size too small.'

'What do you mean? Come on let's see you in it. I'm sure we can sort something out.'

There she was again, the bossy, sniffy saleswoman.

Abigail is bullied into trying it. Huffing and puffing, she struggles to pull the dress down over her various bulges. 'See,' she says sadly, 'I told you it was far too small.' Even so she stares at herself in the mirror, twisting and turning, holding in her breath and straightening her back. Pulling a face she asks plaintively, 'Do you think I could get away with it?'

Her daughter's reply is not encouraging. She nods, 'I'm not so sure. You are right. It is far too small. It's especially tight over your rear end; actually makes it look bigger than it really is.'

Abigail wants to scream, 'Stop right there. Enough with the criticism.' But she holds back. Bonding with Hannah is very rare these days.

Hannah though is in full *helpful* mode. 'Mum if you're asking me to be truly honest, I think you actually look positively uncomfortable in it.' Before Abigail has a chance to, Hannah shouts, 'Don't do that! Don't sit down. Seriously all the seams will pop and we'll have a nightmare getting it off you.' It crosses Hannah's mind she may have been just a little too honest with her opinions, so she backtracks, 'At least, that's what I think. But I'm just a kid, what do I know?'

'Thanks.' Abigail is wondering if she should give some advice about Hannah's bluntness. It's a good way to lose friends.

Her expression must have given her away because Hannah says, 'You don't have to give me a dirty look, you did ask me what I thought. Seeing as you did ask my opinion may I say you're trying too hard? If I was the *person, this Caroline,* whom we both now obviously despise, I'd look at you in that dress and feel pretty smug that you'd gone to all the bother of impressing me.'

Hannah dives into the wardrobe looking through the remainder of the clothes hanging and pulls out a patchwork waistcoat still with its labels attached. 'See now this would work with everything, great with jeans, trousers, or even a skirt. This would be my choice.'

Abigail scrunches up her face and says dismissively, 'No, better not.'

'What do you mean "better not"? Oh God, Mum, don't tell me you nicked it? Is that why all the labels are still on it?' She looks animated and says, 'Wow, are you a shoplifter all of a sudden because if you are there's this blouse I saw in—'

Horrified, Abigail says vehemently, 'No I am not a shoplifter. What the hell's the matter with you? Just because your father's left me doesn't mean to say I'm off the wall nuts.'

Having performed a rerun of all the clothes piled on the bed and come to exactly the same conclusion as she had done half an hour before, Abigail begrudgingly bends to her daughter's suggestion and teams the waistcoat with a pair of cream trousers and a plain cream silk blouse.

'There,' says Hannah in her expanding patronising tone, smoothing down the waistcoat at the back, running her finger down the creases of the trousers in the front in true shop-assistant style. She says, 'See, that's *much* better. Definitely you. Not too showy or too young. Ladies of your age have to be careful not to look mutton-dressed-as-spring-lamb. I see it all the time in the magazines— abandoned women desperate to recapture their lost youth in an attempt to attract new lovers.' Abigail stares at her, not quite knowing what to say to her teenager with her braced teeth and disguised acne. Her totally undiplomatic daughter.

Hannah cups her elbow with one hand, rubbing her chin with the other, head on one side, and says, 'I have to admit Mum, Dad dumping you has done wonders for your figure. You look pretty sensational.'

A compliment? Abigail is not sure but decides to take it. She needs it these days. It gives her a little more confidence as she steps into her car slightly confused but hopefully looking reasonably good. But as she drives through the suburban roads which eventually roll out into the countryside where Zandra's Georgian mansion is situated, Abigail's confidence in her outfit, her straightened hair, her general demeanour starts to slide down into the mire once more. After all, what did her teenage daughter, hardly a woman of the world and just a kid, know about fashion and trying to create an aura of natural sophistication and *who-gives-a-damn*?

The rain is getting heavier now and the windscreen wipers are on full. Abigail is finding it difficult to drive. Mindful of the need to suddenly brake, she is hanging back from the car in front even though the driver behind her is finding this irritating. She waves at him to back off. This gesture seems to annoy him even more and all she can see in her rear-view mirror is his headlights blinding her. She curses Zandra for pushing her into doing something her whole instinct told her was doomed to failure. Now to crown it all she is the potential victim of road rage in a thunderstorm.

The road bends and the impatient road-hog behind suddenly pulls out causing her and the unsuspecting driver in front to swerve. Somehow there is no collision but the shot of adrenalin to the heart is massive. Strangely it helps.

She yells out, 'Sod you Caroline.' She punches the radio on and laughs as the tune playing is, 'I will survive.' She sings at the top of her voice banging the steering wheel at times in tune to the beat.

In her peripheral vision Abigail is aware of the patchwork waistcoat. Like the red dress she had planned to wear, it too has a designer label but also carries another label, one of disillusion, betrayal and finality. That label was the reason Abigail found herself so reticent in choosing it. The unexpected discovery of the beribboned box hidden in the back of her husband's section of the wardrobe was the final nail in their marriage coffin.

When she'd first found it, Abigail had been excited beyond belief. How wonderful to think Baz had bought her a surprise present when there was no birthday or anniversary celebration nearby. It was so out of character. Something he hadn't done in years. Maybe there was hope for them both after all. Particularly as this coincided with his continual absences from home. It seemed there were fewer and fewer occasions when their paths crossed. But as the days wore on and the package hadn't budged an inch from its hidey-hole, Abigail became impatient for it to be handed over to her. What was he waiting for? Was its destiny to be a reward for an extra especially nice Sunday lunch?

One night her mostly no-show husband had rung to say that yet again he was working late at the office and would probably sleep on the couch there. Abigail's curiosity about him and the package had been pushed into overdrive. She lay in the bed tossing and turning wondering exactly what he was doing and with whom? Her insides had been in turmoil. The bed had turned into concrete. Her pillows the same. Her legs were restless, she was hot then cold, hot, cold, uncomfortable and totally wide awake. The hours ticked by. The minutes ticked by. The seconds ticked by. And all the time the box seemed to be calling out for her to discover its contents.

She'd slid out of bed. Nervously checked and rechecked the curtains were drawn tight shut. Desperate not to be discovered in her snooping, she had even gone downstairs to make sure the front door was locked and bolted in case Baz changed his mind, arrived home and caught her red-handed. She'd crept back up the stairs and pulled out the parcel. She stared at it. Rattled it. Poked it. Debated if it was possible the wrapping would come loose accidently on purpose. Finally, she'd given in. The ribbons were a nightmare to undo without damaging them but she'd managed it. She'd carefully pulled off the sticky circular plastic tabs fastening down the lid without making so much as the slightest tear then gingerly she'd opened the box. Whatever secret the box contained it was being cossetted by pure white tissue again fastened by a circular stick-on label. Abigail didn't recognise the brand name. Inside the tissue was the designer patchwork waistcoat and an envelope addressed to someone called Rebecca.

It was as if she had been turned to stone. Or was it jelly? She felt she had no control of her limbs. She was transfixed. Abigail felt as if she was in another dimension. It was almost an out-of-body experience. It wasn't pleasant. There was no triumph in the realisation that all her doubts and fears had been transformed into reality. All those excuses she had made to bolster up her anxieties over his absences were all to no avail. There was no stepping back in time. This was a hard fact which was impossible to ignore. At first, she'd felt unable to breath. Her blood pressure had risen off the scale. The next minute her body was shaking with the shock. She felt icy cold as if her heart was being held tight by an ice monster's hand, its bony fingers digging into her very soul. That heart which until five minutes beforehand had held so much love in it for her husband was now coldly pounding, loudly enough that she thought she was going to have a stroke there and then and die on the spot. Who would find her the next day slumped over the box with the waistcoat? Her daughter Hannah? Or would it be Baz her worthless cheating husband? What would he think? Would he shed a tear? Would he have any regret? Somehow, she didn't think so. Would he be pleased? Would he think smugly, *Well, that saved a bundle of cash on a divorce?'*

With trembling hands, she took the note and punished her tortured mind even more by reading it.

'Darling Rebecca, I saw this and immediately thought of you. Remember Venice and that steamy, glorious night on the canal when we paid the boatman to look away?'

That was it then?

She'd been a mug. She'd been lied to and had swallowed every lie. All the pointers and suspicions recently that Baz was sleeping with someone else which she had chosen to explain away and ignore, well they were all true. Like a lightning bolt from the sky all the jigsaw pieces started to meld together into a horrible life-changing image. She recalled the weekend she and Hannah had spent in Scotland with her grandmother. Baz had been uncontactable. His phone had rung out constantly, his excuse the usual *No signal, love, internet problems, what can you do?* Overwhelmingly, heart-in-mouth, she now realised why. He couldn't be available to make or receive phone calls because the foreign dial-tone would have been a dead giveaway. Besides, he had no need for it while he was having fun with his girlfriend.

At first Abigail's immediate reaction was to ring him there and then, wake him up, wherever he was and scream down the phone at him but it was unlikely he'd answer if his phone was even switched on. She knew she would end up pressing redial over and over and over again, adding to the humiliation.

Instead, she repackaged everything as it was and stuck it back into place. He could keep his low-life secret intact as far as she was concerned. She lay on the bed but there was no way she could fall asleep. She had suspected he had been cheating on her, but now, with proof, her mind had gone nuclear. Images of passion such as she used to enjoy with her husband were replaced by the imagined body of Rebecca. It was an assault to her brain. Was she blonde? Brunette? Redhead? Young? An hour-glass figure with huge breasts? Perfectly rounded bottom and long never-ending legs? Visions of him writhing with this Rebecca woman made her sick to her stomach. Exhausted she finally drifted off only then to experience torturously vivid nightmares where this Rebecca person was naked beneath the fancy gifted waistcoat and her husband.

Her anger suddenly took hold of her. How dare he, how dare he do this to her? How could he have insinuated she was insane with her accusations when all the time her instincts had been bang on. He wasn't just cheating on her but also on his daughter, his beloved Hannah. How could he be so very cruel? She hated him for that, she hated and despised him more than anything or anyone else in the whole of her life. She cried tears of rage alongside tears of hurt and pain. Of betrayal and spent love. And flashes of happier times kept annoyingly hitting her brain. Questions. Why? Why? Why? Had she been such a bad wife, a lover, a friend, that he felt no qualms about having done this to her? Did he have no conscience or guilt in his treacherous cheating body?

Didn't look like it.

At 5 am she said to herself *Sod it, the cow Rebecca can have my worthless husband but she's not getting the Venetian reminder. I'll cut it up or burn it before that happens.*

Having previously undone the package carefully and then even more carefully put it back together, this time she ripped the packaging apart and tore it into tiny pieces. Her rage consuming her. She was about to do the same with the waistcoat but then something stopped her. She googled the brand and was horrified to discover exactly how much he'd spent on it. And therefore, on her! The harlot. The slut. The whore. The husband stealer. The bitch.

She visualised his face when she confronted him with his infidelity. She could hear his protestations, his feeble excuses, see his fake imploring eyes. His stories had always sounded so believable and with foundation that he could turn her suspicions into paranoia. But how could he deny hard fact? A waistcoat! A written note!

Abigail stuffed the note into the front slip pocket of the waistcoat and stuck it on a hanger shoving it into her section of the wardrobe. She was desperate for him to notice it, to see the expression on his face when he realised the game was finally up.

Somehow the following day through grim determination as Abigail applied her make-up, she fixed a smile on her face. She tried to act normally as if it were an ordinary carefree day, dropping off her daughter at school and then onward to work. She'd found it hard to concentrate. She was still nauseous from the sleepless night. She couldn't eat. All the time she was continually thinking ahead to the evening when she would demand an explanation, planning her action, formulating her speeches. Absurdly she had to suffer a longer wait for her unfaithful husband as he didn't arrive back for another two days. When he finally turned up, she was ill-prepared. Words, speeches, actions, all forgotten. As much as she tried, her rehearsed plan of action could not be retrieved from her grief-stricken mind.

Luckily, Hannah was staying overnight with a friend when Abigail walked through the front door to find her husband sitting there with his coat on in the dark drinking coffee and smoking.

'Oh, you're home then,' she'd said, coldly.

'Bit obvious. Yes, I'm home.'

'And smoking! Hmm, what a surprise! Thought you sworn you'd given that up for good?' she'd added, even more icily.

'So did I.' He'd then lit another with the smouldering almost spent cigarette defiantly, taunting her to make another comment and said, 'Circumstances.'

'Circumstances? That's what you call it.'

Abigail's heart was thumping. She had rage but she also had fear, anxiety, terror. The terror of suddenly being alone in the world with Hannah minus support, especially financial support. She was at that point of no return that so many marriages encounter when a confrontation would mean the total collapse and end of the alliance. Once those words, those accusations had been spoken and were out in the ether for all to hear, there was no way back. No time-machine. No replay-button. Many times she'd bitten her tongue, wary of such a finality because of Hannah. But Hannah was now fifteen. Which was worse, her living in a household of lies and deceit *with* her father or in a hopefully more harmonious atmosphere where maybe money would be tight, the house might be sold, but her life might be more honest? It was an almost impossible choice. Did she have the courage to make that decision? Would she allow *circumstances* to drift along so that it wouldn't be her decision but that of her husband's?

With hesitation devouring her, Abigail bit her tongue. Those previous days and nights of anguish choked her, stuck in her throat like an oversized pill that was hard to swallow. She debated with herself if she was doing the right thing. Maybe this was yet another fling which would run its course; had run its course just like all the others. She'd been accused of over-reacting enough times before. Maybe she had driven Baz to these lengths because of her mistrust of him all these years.

Then she spotted the suitcase by the door. She was puzzled at first and then angry. She felt like a fool. He'd come home to pack for probably another jolly jaunt with *Rebecca*. Ugh, how she hated that name. She'd known a couple of Rebecca's in her life. One was at school. Becky. Horrible, nasty, trouble-making Becky. There was the one at work in her first job, Becca. Too posh to make the tea for everyone. And now *her*, the husband thief.

'I'm leaving you.'

Just like that. He'd said it just like that!

'What?' She couldn't have heard him correctly. She must have imagined the words.

'You heard. I'm leaving you. OK?' he'd said.

There was silence. Hanging there between them like a hovering wasp, its venom pointing in both directions.

'Leaving me?' she'd said. 'Yeah, I heard the words. I just don't believe them. *You* are leaving *me?* That's rich, that's so up-your-arse rich! How about I'm throwing you out instead?'

He hadn't looked around, drawing down on the cigarette to take a long hit of nicotine and shrugged, 'Suit yourself. Same difference.' The words had been uttered in a monotone. A throw-away line as if he didn't care. Had never cared. She was incensed.

The avalanche of hurt began slowly and then built at speed. Everything came spilling out, the years of angst, nights of no sleep, the worry of STDs, the betrayal of her and his daughter; it was endless. A veritable tsunami of words she let loose, the dam of torture that had been stored inside her had burst. It should have been a relief, the fact she'd held back, churning the words and thoughts inside her for all those years. Yet it wasn't. It was all out now. All said. No pulling back. No change of heart from either party. The die had been cast. She was empty, hollow, vacant, drained.

What did Baz do?

Nothing.

He sat there listening. Then slowly stubbed out his cigarette. Stood up, pushed her to one side, gently manhandling her shoulders so he could get past. Picked up his suitcase and walked through the front door without a backward glance. He didn't slam the door but pulled it to, so quietly Abigail wasn't convinced he'd even shut it.

Abigail had stood still with silent tears falling down her cheeks thick and fast, her knees trembling, her whole body shaking. She felt weak and unable to stand. She'd slumped to the floor in a heap, almost in a foetal position. Abigail must have stayed like that for a good ten minutes before it hit her that her marriage was definitely over and there was no way back for either of them even if they'd wanted one.

Afterwards she'd wondered why she hadn't even asked him to stay, or for an explanation as to why he was leaving? And who was Rebecca? And how long had this affair been going on? And what was he going to say to Hannah? And what about the house? And the mortgage? And—and—and—and, so many ands, so many things, and now he was gone, with no answers, no explanations, no sign of remorse, or apologies.

Nothing.

Silence.

Coldness.

Disconnected.

Abigail was distraught. So many questions left unanswered. No answers to so many questions. So much hurt, so much pain that when Hannah came home Abigail didn't know what to tell her.

'Fancy a take-out tonight love?' she'd asked, trying to control the tremble in her voice.

'Take-out? What on a Wednesday? Did we win the lottery or something?'

Then Abigail had broken down. Hannah knew immediately. She didn't need any explanation. She was a bright thing. 'Don't worry Mum, we'll manage until Dad sees sense and comes back.'

How could she tell Hannah he wasn't coming back? She knew deep down he never would. Anyway, she didn't want him back. Or did she? Abigail was in a torment of mixed feelings. Before all she could think of was his moodiness and no-shows at school events; his lack of support when she needed it most; his increasing absences. Now, all the memories were good ones, of laughter, fun and stupidity, of times when she believed nothing could end their love for each other and nothing could ever destroy them. But it had.

That was four months ago. Discussions were since directed through solicitors. Hannah had seen her father a couple of times and a couple of times he hadn't shown. But the waistcoat was still here. That hadn't moved out. It symbolised everything about her marriage, hanging there, taunting her. Until Hannah pulled it off the rail and told Abigail to try it on.

It would puzzle Abigail from time to time afterwards why she had let Hannah persuade her into wearing the wretched thing. Most people, she thought, would have had the sense to tear it to shreds or at least give it to a charity shop, or tried to sell it on eBay. But somehow the designer waistcoat was an important symbol. One of defiance. Yes, maybe Rebecca had won her husband form her but then again maybe she hadn't won anything. Maybe they hadn't even been an item and Abigail's assumption had been wrong. Or if they were together, they weren't now. Who knew and who cared? But Abigail, like the song on the radio said, was a survivor and survivors used every weapon they could lay their hands on. The waistcoat in a peculiar way, was the colourful expensive statement Abigail needed to keep that said she didn't care about being deserted by a worthless man.

So, she was trying to wear it proudly. It was original. It was expensive. It was hers, now, because Rebecca could never receive it. It was a small victory and she would use it to fortify herself against the no doubt oncoming onslaught of Caroline and her continuing, unexplained vendetta against Abigail and her friends.

CHAPTER FOUR

The group of women are sitting in front of a roaring fire, candles everywhere, but not from choice. They are suffering the fourth power cut in as many hours. 'Good job you decided to do a cheese fondue Zandra. You must have known somehow.'

'Not really. It was simply Cook's day off today—visiting her mother in Maidstone.'

'How many *staff* do you have here nowadays Zandra?' asks Victoria trying not to sound too judgemental. Victoria is very down to earth and doesn't approve of people *doing* things for folk. She says she's a socialist but probably her beliefs are more hard-line than mere socialism. Although Zandra is a bit of an exception she'll admit. She's her pal. Come the Revolution, if it comes in her life-time, she won't be the one sent to the Guillotine with the old lady sitting outside knitting, or be condemned to spend the rest of her days in rotting prison without her Chanel or lip-gloss.

Victoria is a tall rather lumpy woman and sits awkwardly perched on the end of an overstuffed chair by the fireplace. She is of ruddy complexion and suffers fearfully with varicose veins. She was the seventh child to be born into a family of six brothers. Instead of being cossetted and spoilt, as one would imagine for an only girl, due to her build and plain appearance she was regarded as being yet another male in the family, a weaker version than her brothers. What made matters even worse was that when her mother died a year later in child birth her father proved to be totally dysfunctional as a parent. He had no conception of bringing up children, let alone a girl and relied solely on the older boys to help out. Until Victoria went to school, she wore nothing but hand-me-downs from her siblings and was happy to do so. She spent her first day at school hiding in the shrubbery embarrassed that she was wearing a skirt and not trousers.

It took her over three decades to finally admit her sexuality, which occasionally when inebriated she blames on her upbringing. Her drunken bouts can descend into practically paralytic proportions. In those times she tediously explains to anyone who mishappens to be propping up the bar next to her, 'See, if my mother hadn't have died so early and if I'd had a sister or an aunt or a friendly female neighbour, things might have been different. You've no idea how difficult life has been.'

Her friends knew how difficult life had been. Victoria had told them, over and over again *exactly* how difficult life had been until Abigail had been commissioned by the others to have a gentle word with her. Abigail had little idea why Victoria would listen to her advice over anyone else's but assumed she'd been nominated because she was the oldest of the group. Now that Zandra's bath-time revelation all has become clear and slotted perfectly into place, Abigail makes a mental note to be wary of extended hugs from Victoria.

Abigail was not the only one to give out advice. Saoirse, the youngest of the group, would point out from time to time to her sad-faced friend, 'Life's not a bed of roses for anyone Victoria. At least you've never had to put up with bullies with all of your brothers there to protect you.'

Victoria, who now insists on being called Vic, has been debating recently whether to go the whole hog and transform herself into a bearded male with no way back. With her visits to the gym and bodybuilding she certainly has the physique for an easy transformation. Disadvantages weigh heavily against the advantages. One disadvantage is her life-long friendship with *the gang* as she now calls them. She is overly anxious that turning male would be considered as having joined ranks with the *enemy*. It isn't so much that the girls mostly regard all men as untrustworthy individuals but the conversations almost always lead to some male's actions being vilified, their personality decried or ridiculed, or both, and their time on planet earth being questioned as to its viability as their words, actions and lives are torn apart by the vulturous females.

Victoria, Vic, remains part of their scene even if she doesn't always agree with their aspersions on the male sex. She doesn't want that aspect of her life to change yet. She doesn't want to become the outsider. But the vibe is there, so when the girls want to discuss the latest male villain, they mostly choose a moment when Victoria's isn't around.

Life undercover of a closeted lesbian had almost forced her to end her life as a teenager. It was the year before the girls were due to leave the security of their school and make their way out into the world. At that time, Victoria had become, due to stress, thin, flat-chested with stick legs and arms to match. She became embarrassed when the other girls talked about boyfriends and what stage they were at with them. Her father had banned her from boys until at least she had secured a real nine-to-five job, like a proper adult woman would do.

Caroline decided Victoria's father was wrong about everything.

She arranged to give Victoria a push in the right direction. She might have had good motives but it remained debatable.

Two things happened in fairly quick succession which nearly pushed Victoria over the edge. The first was that she had a massive crush on one of the teachers. The young woman who was not much older than the group was a Miss Wiggins, their English and Form teacher. Wiggy, as she was nicknamed, was just out of training college. She wore her long golden hair loose which framed her heart-shaped features. Wiggy was stunning and everyone loved her. Victoria was *in love* with her. She hung on her every word in lesson time. When homework was writing poetry, Victoria wrote a love poem— with Wiggy as her muse. Not that Wiggy cottoned on, thankfully.

Victoria was always game for a dare and when Caroline suggested when on blackboard cleaning duty in class that Victoria should unobtrusively snip a trophy lock off Wiggy's hair, she couldn't wait. Wiggy's hair! What a wonderful thought. What a fantastic keepsake of love! That very birthday, a month earlier, her father had given her the locket her mother had bequeathed her. And now she would have something significant to put in it. Next to her heart. She would wear it always.

Abigail and Saoirse were dead against the idea. 'Don't do it Victoria. This will go horribly wrong. What if you get expelled?' 'What if you end up at Mannington Secondary? It's *awful* there? The food is disgusting.' 'What if old mother Sherman finds out?' Old mother Sherman was Miss Sherman, the headmistress, a terrifying character on normal days but when there was a castigation to be done, punishment was a no holds barred exercise, designed to create memories to be haunted by.

Victoria had quaked slightly at all these thoughts and threats but the overwhelming desire to have something of her favourite teacher, her mentor, her non-participating lover, well it was too hard not to comply with the challenge Caroline had set down.

The morning came. Word had spread around the class what Victoria was going to do. There was a veritable buzz of excitement in the air. Wiggy looked at them all as she finished the roll call, her expression one of puzzlement. She obviously sensed some plot and demanded of them, 'What are you girls up to? Whatever it is, I suggest you change your minds.' Although she was a novice, she had enough of a nose for naughtiness to realise they were planning something bad.

The desks were in rows and Caroline was sitting behind Victoria. She prodded her back with her with the end of her ruler and said, 'Go on Victoria, what are you waiting for?'

'Line up for assembly please,' said Wiggy. The moment had passed. There was a tangible choral sigh of disappointment and disillusionment alongside a fair degree of relief for Victoria.

'Thought you had some guts,' said one. 'Cowardy-custard,' muttered another. And so on.

Victoria drifted through the morning session waiting for the inevitable criticism from all at lunch-time, particularly from Caroline. She was not wrong in that. Caroline made a bee-line for her and launched into her assessment of Victoria's inability to carry out a simple dare. 'Always thought you were a coward. You with all your brothers. God, don't make me laugh,' she went on, dragging in anyone she could to join in the humiliation and ridicule of Victoria until the poor girl lapsed into a verge of tears.

There was nothing for it. Back from lunch, and back into their classroom for an afternoon of English with Wiggy.

Wiggy looked at the blackboard with its list of French verbs from the morning classwork and beckoned to Victoria, 'Come on Victoria! You're blackboard monitor this week. Do your job, please.'

Normally, on hearing her name called by Wiggy, she'd have been instantly thrown into a good-humoured whirl but this time it plunged her into a sense that she was about to self-destruct. Nudged again by Caroline and facially urged on by some of the others, Victoria made her way up to the front of the class.

'I realise it's not on our curriculum girls but today we're going to discuss an extract of Crime and

Punishment. Pass these around would you please, Victoria.'

Victoria sighed with relief. A reprieve. She had something else to do. Then Wiggy turned to her, 'Blackboard Victoria, don't forget.'

Victoria started to rub hard at the blackboard, aware of all the eyes behind her watching in anticipation. She had the scissors in her school skirt pocket. She finished cleaning the board desperately trying not to cough with all the chalk dust. She turned around and there was Wiggy, head bent forward peering over the sheets of paper in front of her. Taking a deep breath, she pulled out the scissors and leant forward, gently lifting one thin section of hair, and was about to snip when Caroline knocked over her wooden pencil case. The noise startled Wiggy so much she leapt up to find Victoria tugging at her hair. Then she screamed.

The class erupted into disorder. The noise was almost deafening. It was inevitable old mother Sherman would hear.

Victoria was given a week's detention. She denied that anyone else was involved. Victoria was no grass, no sneak, no tell-tale tit. Caroline assumed the role of well-intentioned friend, pretending to be mortified and assured everyone, 'It was a *total* accident, I'm so sorry.'

One person was doubtful that Caroline meant no harm. Abigail.

The second incident was only a month later. Caroline had wanted to, 'Make it up to you, Victoria, for that dreadful, dreadful incident.' It came after a fortnight of concentrated mickey-taking on Caroline's part. Allegedly it was meant to be light-hearted to those around, even so, Caroline was told firmly to back-off by Abigail and Saoirse. Her reply, 'Why, it's all in good part isn't it, Victoria?' who feeling hounded, nodded in agreement. Victoria always felt in awe of Caroline. Others might have called it *intimidated*.

The mickey-taking was about Victoria's boy-like figure and her flat chest. 'When are you going to grow boobs like the rest of us. You haven't even got pimples?' Or 'Have you ordered your breasts yet, is that what you asked Santa for?' Or 'Is that you Steven?' Steven was Victoria's elder brother, by a year. 'Oh, no, it is you, Victoria. Sorry, my mistake.' The cruellest one was when Caroline began to call her *Peanuts*. And so the jibes went on, tiresomely and hurtfully.

Caroline had a succession of boyfriends and friends who had boyfriends. She organised a gathering. It was a snogging session although Victoria wasn't to know that until she arrived. Caroline's parents had gone out for the evening. The teenagers had the run of the place.

It all appeared to be quite civilised at first. Victoria was introduced to Henry, Caroline's cousin, a tall shy young man who blushed each time Victoria spoke to him, which was infrequent. He was full of spots which he'd tried to hide by attempting to grow his first beard, the result resembling a mouldy potato covered in small plasters where he'd cut himself with the razor.

There were six couples in all. At first Victoria sat meekly next to Henry trying to make conversation. 'What subjects are you doing for your GCSE's?'

Having exhausted the subject of school she asked him, 'Do you play games?'

Apparently not.

Henry was neither academic, nor sporty, nor arty, or anything else really. He was probably the mirror image of Victoria: shy and unable to converse easily with the opposite sex. She had all but given up and was looking at her watch, about to suggest she needed to get home, when Caroline anticipating her exit announced, 'OK guys, it's game time.'

Initially it was musical chairs. Victoria was surprised at Caroline's choice but felt it fairly innocuous until she realised it wasn't just the chairs that were involved it was the boys. The boys sat on all the chairs and then when the music stopped, the girls had to sit on the nearest boy's lap. Caroline had obviously planned it so Victoria would end up with Henry.

'Right, you're out Victoria,' she said gleefully quickly stopping Victoria from moving. 'No Victoria. Stay there. You've still got to sit on his lap until the game ends.'

Victoria didn't know who was more embarrassed, her or Henry. It was apparent that neither party had sat on or been sat on before and Henry's body responded accordingly. Victoria found it unpleasant and disturbing. Even being brought up with seven males in the house hadn't prepared her for her first sexual encounter.

'Now,' said Caroline, 'it's our old favourite, spin the bottle.'

Mysteriously, Victoria again won Henry.

'Off you go.' It was a big house and there were half a dozen bedrooms. 'Any bedroom that's vacant, take your pick.'

It was all too much for Victoria. 'Sorry Henry, not feeling too good,' she said, face reddened. 'Have to go home.'

'I'll take you.'

Worried that his delivery of her home would warrant a prize she didn't want to give, she declined until he insisted. 'It's OK, I'm only walking you home that's all, don't worry.'

On the Monday morning came the finger pointing and uncontrollable sniggering behind Victoria's back. 'Bet she's a lezza,' one of them snorted. 'She didn't snog Henry. Told you she was gay.'

Victoria was horrified. She wanted to be normal. Didn't normal people have crushes on teachers? Surely they did? Did all teenage girls *have* to have boyfriends before they wanted to? Then there was the worry of her father. If he'd found out about the snogging party, he would have gone apeshit. All Victoria wanted was to be was a normal person, a normal girl. There was never any notion or inner thought she might be different.

The humiliation and ridicule lasted all week even though Abigail and Saoirse tried to assure her it didn't matter and not to listen to it. Caroline pretended she wasn't involved in any of the mickey taking. She even tried to convince her it had all been a horrible mistake and she'd only been trying to get her a boyfriend just so she wouldn't feel so out place. But Victoria detected little real sincerity from her.

The problem was, was that no amount of reassurance from Abigail and Saoirse was going to be enough to quell the overwhelming feeling of disgust and dismay she was suffering inside.

It was 2am when her eldest brother, Sean, found Victoria vomiting in the bathroom. She'd left a note explaining her actions and then taken what she had assumed, as described on the bottle, was a pile of aspirins. Except it wasn't a bottle of aspirin, ironically it was a bottle of anti-nausea pills which were relatively innocuous anyway.

A shaking and distraught Sean sat her down and talked to her man to man, he said. He tried to instil in her that nothing was worth doing anything as crazy as taking a bunch of pills. Nothing. And no-one. Victoria never got over the two humiliations, even though she pretended to accept that Caroline's part in them was purely innocent. But they left scars which never healed. No more was Victoria in awe of Caroline. Instead, sewn were the beginnings of a building grudge.

A month or so later Caroline tentatively attempted to see if Victoria had forgiven her by joking, 'Funny the book old Wiggy gave us was Crime and Punishment, wasn't it?'

Victoria had laughed. But it was a hollow one.

***

The friends are seated at a largish table which they have dragged in from another room. Zandra's idea as, 'There doesn't seem much point in lighting another fire when we're all so cosy in here, does there?'

In the middle of the table is the fondue bowl surrounded by small chunks of bread.

'Get stuck in ladies.'

There is the usual *no, after you*, and *sorry, did I just knock your bread off?* with increasing giggles as more and more wine is consumed than is probably necessary to wash down the calorific mixture of melted gruyere and gouda.

'Good job no-one's driving home, isn't it?' says Saoirse.

Abigail was relieved that her daughter had already planned to overnight with a friend She didn't want to be forced back out into that storm. Zandra suggested everyone should stay, in view of how dangerous it looked outside. It was a fairly easy decision to make. The journey to Zandra's house was definitely not something she wanted to repeated tonight in reverse, not in the dark, and not when the local news outlets were saying most of the roads were now under water.

Although for Abigail it is difficult to put out of her mind the uncomfortable fact that the storm meant she would be spending the night in the same house as Caroline.

She glances at her companions, none of them seem bothered by Caroline being there, in fact it's almost the opposite. They all appear to have accepted her back into the fold as if Caroline had never done any harm to any of them.

For Abigail, the strangest thing she notices is Saoirse's unexpected warmth towards Caroline. She, the poor girl, more than all of them was undoubtedly hurt the most, although there was no vying for the top of Caroline's hit list. It was true that Abigail's marriage had a major wrecking ball aimed at it by Zandra before it had even begun but at least she could counterbalance that by having enjoyed some happy times with Baz. Plus, there was the bonus of their daughter, Hannah. But Saoirse? How different her life might have been without Caroline's meddling participation.

Abigail thinks back to the time. Four of the gang had decided on further education, Gwen opting for a different college from the other three. Zandra had never intended to waste time learning useless stuff than was necessary. She had no need. Her parents could provide for her until Zandra had found a suitable man or they had found one for her. By the time they were leaving school Victoria had made the decision to join the Army, figuring she'd fit in better there than anywhere else.

After the first year of living in Halls, the threesome, Caroline, Abigail and Saoirse, had rented a house nearer the sea than the college. They studied on the beach. They ate on the beach. They played on the beach. They fell in love and then out of love, on the beach. The beach was their life. When they weren't studying, they busked, mostly on the beach during busy sunny days, but otherwise in the town, in fact anywhere to get extra money for food, clothes and occasionally marijuana. They called themselves the Three Busketeers. They became so popular that soon local pubs were hiring them on a Friday night. They even managed to be the star attraction at a wedding party. Good music *and* pretty faces. It was a knock-out combination.

No-one could divide them. They were inseparable. At times they fell out, as all females do, but the rows were short-lived mostly started by money or the lack of, or men which was of little surprise. The incidents at school and Caroline's involvement, which caused Victoria's cry for help, had been dismissed long ago as her mere misjudging of a situation. If ever it was brought up, tears would spring into Caroline's eyes and bizarrely she'd be cossetted and comforted as if *she'd* been the victim. Such is life, full of strange injustices.

It was Saoirse's idea to busk. Her family were not only musical but theatrical as well. Her great uncle had been a Shakespearean actor, not of any note, but his booming voice and overpowering presence had influenced her decision to take an English and Drama degree. Her idea was not only to be an actress but to write something she could star in, such was her ambition to not only become famous but to earn so much money she could make her parents' lives more comfortable and secure.

From an early age Saoirse had written mini plays dishing out hand-written scripts for her friends in order to perform at Christmastime or birthdays. Her short stories, published in the school magazine, were read by pupils and staff alike. She even won a prize in the local newspaper for a feature about a day in the life of a schoolgirl. She was talented. Everyone, everywhere thought so. She was on her way.

Three years on, the Busketeers' final days at college were fast approaching. Saoirse had planned to go back to Dublin for the summer to catch up with her family before taking a job as a reporter for one of the national papers. She felt this was the best route into this difficult world of words. Be a journalist. Get published in black and white. Get her words down in print for all to see. And then, books, lots and lots of books and plays, working towards her ultimate goal, movies. Everything, though, depended on getting her degree. Her tutors described her as an outstanding student and the projections were always the same—a first. It was virtually guaranteed. Neither Caroline nor Abigail had yet mapped out their own future careers. They were enjoying university life too much to think about it. While Saoirse's plan was rigidly fixed the other two were muting the idea of finding accommodation together in London and then a job of some sort, whatever that might be.

It was the day before Saoirse had to hand in her two dissertations. She'd spent hours writing them, revamping them, honing them. For years she had bashed out her stories on an old Olympia typewriter and she'd seen no reason to change to a computer. Then heart-breaking news came. A phone call. Her father was gravely ill in hospital, having suffered a stroke. Her mother needed her desperately. There was no time to think straight. She placed both dissertations in their respective envelopes. Caroline was there to help. She volunteered to personally deliver them to the college.

'Now you won't forget? You realise you're holding my future life in your hands here, Caro?'

'Course not. Don't worry I'll do it first thing before anything else. Before I've even had breakfast. Trust me.'

Saoirse had thought no more about it. She didn't have time. Her mother was in pieces and she figured that when the hospital released her father there would be no-one but her available to nurse both of them back to good health.

A week or so later, one of her parents' neighbours was waiting for her on the door step as she got back from another bedside vigil. It was Mrs O'Riordan. 'Sure, I hope you won't being taking offence Saoirse darling,' she said, 'but your phone's being ringing and ringing off the hook all afternoon and I couldn't stand it no more. Your mother gave me a key years ago and so I hope you don't mind but I let myself in and answered it. Here, I've written the name and number down for you. He says could you phone him back today please. It's urgent.'

It was from Mr McTavish, her landlord. Her heart sank. More problems on top of what was already going on. Either the other two had gone and left her with a bunch of bills to pay or he was moaning about the wretched stain on the living room carpet. She cursed both of them as she dialled the number and then stopped. Did she really need that on top of everything else she was dealing with? Saoirse walked into the kitchen and put the kettle on. Her mother was staying by her father's bedside that afternoon and Saoirse was glad of the break. She had just poured the boiling water into the cup when the phone rang again. She had to answer it in case it was the hospital but it wasn't. It was Mr McTavish.

'Hello Mr McTavish. Sorry not to have phoned back. I take it you're phoning about the stain on the carpet in the front room, but can I say, that was there before we—'

'Hold your horses, hen, it's not about the stain, although now you've mentioned it, I'll be taking a good look at that. No, lassie, one of your professors has been pestering the life out of me asking where you are. It's something about a disillusionment or something.'

'Disillusionment? Oh, do you mean dissertation?'

'Aye, that's it. Get a bit tongue-twisted sometimes. He says you've missed the deadline. Told me how you're his brightest student and he couldn't understand why you'd do that. Got his number here somewhere.'

Instantly in a state of panic and anxiety, she fumbled a thank you to Mr McTavish for his kindness. She couldn't understand what could have happened and so she called Caroline. It was a foreign ringtone then diverted to voicemail. She then called Abigail. She picked up.

'Saoirse, is that you? Oh God is everything all right? It isn't your father, is it? I haven't called you because, I haven't wanted to bother you when I know you're up to your eyes in—'

'No, I know, don't worry, I get why you haven't called. Thanks. That's not it. Where's Caroline? I need to talk to her urgently.'

'Er, not sure exactly, somewhere in the Med, I think. Her cousin bought a yacht and she's helping him sail it. Well, that's her story, I reckon that—'

Saoirse isn't interested. 'She didn't hand my dissertations in.'

'What? You're kidding me? She told me she had. She absolutely confirmed 110%.'

'Well, she didn't. I've had McTavish on the phone blathering on about how Steven Bagshaw's been hounding him about where I am. What the hell did she do with them? She promised me faithfully.' Saoirse fought back her tears. 'How could she do this to me? Everything rests on that degree, everything. My life's about to be ruined. All that hard slog for nothing.'

'There has to be a logical reason, surely,' said Abigail. 'Someone in the college has mislaid them. I can't believe Caroline would do that deliberately. Would she?'

Suddenly, though, Victoria's attempted suicide came flooding to mind alongside other hitherto fairly unnoteworthy episodes where Caroline had burst into tears on being challenged for something she'd alleged wasn't designed to upset or hurt anyone.

Abigail, hopeful, asked, 'Did you keep a copy?'

'Yes. But where would it be? You two packed everything up. Do you know?'

'I'll look. I'll get off the phone right away and search through everything. Meantime you get onto Steven Bagshaw, tell him what's happened. Maybe it's not too late.'

'It will be. It has to be. Oh God, I knew I should have handed them in myself but Mum was beside herself and Dad, well, I had to go. I didn't have time.'

'How is he?'

'Hanging on. Somehow.' She paused. 'I know what you're saying that in the big scheme of things Dad's health is more important than—' She paused. 'It's just if I don't get the degree, I won't get the job and they'll ask what happened and I'll have to say that I missed the deadline. Newspapers don't want people who miss deadlines. Would you employ someone who after three years of studying didn't make sure their work got marked? I can't believe this is happening to me. How could she do this? I trusted her.'

'I'm sure we can fix it. Don't worry,' said Abigail with very little confidence that she believed in what she was saying.

No-one ever found the dissertations. Caroline, on her eventual return, bronzed and fit with a new rich boyfriend in tow, assured Saoirse she had definitely handed it in to one of the porters. 'It has to be down to them, not me. I did what you asked truly I did. You've got to believe me. I wouldn't do that to you, Saoirse, you're my friend.' Then came the usual and inevitable sobs and the demand of sympathy for the accused. Caroline could never cogitate the stress and anxiety she caused her victims. She was never wrong and people should really understand how her suffering was at least as bad as Saoirse's, shouldn't they? Could people not see things from her point of view?

Saoirse wasn't able to find work for six months while she was nursemaid to her parents, until her father eventually departed. Her mother pleaded with her to find a job locally until she was strong enough to be left alone. Saoirse resolved that maybe she could never have taken the job she had lost anyway, because of her family tragedy. That didn't mute the anguish that she may now never be considered for any other such jobs in the future. All employers wanted candidates with degrees, not almost degrees. It had become the norm. No-one was going to listen to someone who made excuses about dissertations mysteriously disappearing. Those three university years had been for nothing. Time wasted. And when Saoirse ate the words Caroline served her, she was shocked. *It was fortunate in a way, wasn't it?' said Caroline. 'It saved Saoirse from having to choose between her career and her parents.'* It wasn't for Caroline to decide.

Saoirse was bitter and she had good reason to be. From that time until the fondue party, Saoirse and Caroline hadn't spoken. Caroline had sent Christmas cards, birthday cards and even holiday postcards but it took years before Saoirse reluctantly and definitely with no warm feelings, had returned festive greetings. It had taken up until now for the two to actually utter a word to each other, and for Abigail, it was uncomfortably flowing, as far as she could make out.

It was inexplicable to her that time had magically healed the damage Caroline had done to Saoirse. Caroline had screwed up her life. It wasn't a trivial, *oh these things happen*, event.

'Penny for your thoughts,' asks Victoria, 'you look miles away.'

'Just thinking about old times, you know.'

Zandra says, 'It's a pity Gwen couldn't be here as well. Apparently, her daughter-in-law is giving birth and she's looking after the two-year-old.' She pauses, 'When was the last time we were all together?' she looks directly at Abigail. 'It was your wedding day, wasn't it?'

There is a horrible silence when an image of Caroline and Baz locked together flashes to the front of Abigail's brain. Saoirse, at the same time, is remembering the hurt she felt in having to refuse the invitation because of Caroline's presence at the wedding. Victoria jumps in, realising the evening is about to take a downward dive and says, 'Well, I couldn't get leave. No, I think it was that bank holiday we had just after we'd left school. We were altogether then. Eastbourne, wasn't it?'

Zandra picks up quickly, 'No, it was before spring half term. Hastings, wasn't it? Definitely Hastings, I remember the dodgems. And the weather, oh my God it rained all weekend! And the caravan was rot, wasn't it? Absolutely *not* as was described, so filthy. Ugh. When I told Mummy afterwards what it was like she made me bathe in disinfectant and threw all my clothes in the bin.' Zandra gives an embarrassed laugh.

Saoirse and Abigail are still silent as Zandra and Victoria prattle on about the boys who followed them back to the caravan and wouldn't go away and kept shaking the caravan until they thought it was going to topple over. 'But when we finally gave in them, we had a whale of a time.'

'They bought the beer,' Victoria says.

'And the chips. Goodness, those terribly greasy chips. All that cholesterol, it doesn't bear *thinking* about it now,' Zandra says.

'Who brought the portable CD player with a stack of 45's? Was it you?'

Victoria continues, 'Yeah, I borrowed it from Steven. He gave me hell for that. Do you remember we were all dancing in there? How I don't know when there was absolutely no room in that tiny caravan. I kept bashing into everything. And that old manky couple came banging at the caravan door and—'

Abigail shouts, 'Stop. Stop all this.' She stands up and leans her hands on the table. 'This is all so phoney. So fake. What are we doing, kidding ourselves that nothing's wrong here? How can you, Caroline, sit there and pretend in your holy-than-thou attitude that everything's fine now because you said *sorry*. Well, it's not fine. And you, Victoria, *Vic,* I can't believe you can even *sit* next to her, let alone talk about how much fun we all had. That Hastings holiday was just after you—'

'Please Abigail, you're spoiling the evening.'

Abigail pushes the chair back roughly and says coldly, 'Spoiling the evening, that's some joke. She,' and she points directly at Caroline, 'she has spoilt all of our lives in one way or another.' She mimics Zandra's posh tone, 'I believe Gwen couldn't be here because her daughter-in-law is giving birth. Really? Her daughter-in-law gave birth last month, as well you know. It was an excuse. Something I should have stuck to instead of being privy to this farce of sitting around a bowl of melted cheese, politely chatting about all our wonderful yesterdays. And, by the way, she may have apologised to all of you and you may have gullibly swallowed her crap but has she, or will she apologise to me for what she did to me on my wedding day? How she destroyed it, and me? Answer: no. Of course, she hasn't and she won't.'

Abigail heads for the door. 'I'm taking my chances with the flooded roads. I'm out of here. I can't be in this house one minute longer. I can't breathe in here. This hypocrisy is suffocating me,' she says. 'Sorry Zandra, I know you mean well. You're a good friend but why you're entertaining that evil bitch is beyond me. You've got to be some kind of saint. But I'm not, and never will be. Me, I'm going to revel in being the non-forgiver. I'm going to turn it into an art form. That woman,' and Abigail points to Caroline again, 'is poison through and through, and she will *never, ever* change. Even on her death-bed she'll be plotting with the devil.'

Abigail heads for the kitchen where her clothes are drying. Zandra on her heels behind her says, 'Abby, you can't go, you're well over the limit. Please. It's awful out there.' It is, the storm is still raging against the window, as loudly as it was earlier. It hasn't abated.

'I'm not *that* much over the limit, if at all. Had you been less intent on sucking up to that piece of shit you might have noticed that I've hardly drunk a drop. You forgot to pour. And I was too mindful of not speaking my mind but now I have, so…Sorry to say it again, but if there's one thing in life I can't stand, it's hypocrisy.'

'What are you doing? You can't put wet clothes on, stop for goodness' sake.'

Abigail stops disrobing, 'OK, you're right. I'll shove these in a bag. Have you got a bag?' Zandra hands her a Harrods bag. Abigail has to smile, 'Only you Zandra would give someone a Harrods bag to put their stuff into.' She throws her arms around her and says sorrowfully, 'I'm sorry I ruined your evening. I couldn't hold back anymore. Life's shit at the moment and she was just one step too far.'

Strangely as Abigail steps out into the night the rain stops, probably not for long but it is a pause in the weather. She looks up. The sky is a lot brighter now, black clouds scudding across the moon. She shivers. It is eerie to say the least. She has unlocked the car door and is about to step in when she hears footsteps behind her.

She turns saying, 'It's no good Zandra, you can't persuade me to—'

'Leaving on my account? Should I be flattered? My God, you must absolutely hate me to risk your life driving through flooded roads. Oh, and by the way, compliments on your sewing. How clever of you to make that little patchwork number. I suppose nowadays it's what you have to do with hardly any money coming in. Or did you pick it from the local hospice shop?'

'Bitch! It was designer, as well you know.'

'You don't say! Thought it seemed familiar. But before you go, a little home truth for you Abigail, just to put the record straight. Your husband, Baz, and I were an item long before you were ever considered on the marriage spectrum as far as he was concerned. Basically, you were a rebound. I don't suppose he told you that I'd ditched him the night before he proposed to you?'

'What's rubbish. We'd been together a year before he proposed. You're lying, as usual and you're really bad at it, Caroline, always were.'

Caroline folds her arms. 'Really? You think so?' she quizzes. 'Well, here's something you don't know. For your information you may have been out on dates but he was in my bed most nights after seeing you and always on the nights he told you he was *going to football practice* or *having a pint with the boys* or particularly the week you'd bought tickets for Glastonbury. Remember then? We had a holiday in Greece. You're a sad little fool, you were at school, and you still are. You're pathetic. Mooning over a man who was never yours. I'm amazed your marriage lasted as long as it did and it only did because I didn't want him. And always you thought we were best friends. What a joke! What a fool you are.'

'Piss off.'

'Nice language. But as you wind your merry way home to your soon-to-be-sold house before you get kicked out, consider this: You think he was having an affair with someone called Rebecca, don't you? Think again. That's my *middle* name.' Caroline smirks. 'Now, off you go! Don't crash or do anything stupid, will you? Do drive carefully. Remember the floods. I'd hate for anything to happen to you, like being drowned in a ditch as no-one will look for you. You're a lost cause.'

Abigail gets into the car. Her whole body is trembling with rage. Somehow, she manages to start the engine without stalling it and reverses the car at speed doing a perfect three-point-turn and regardless of Zandra's carefully raked gravel, shoves her foot down hard on the accelerator, hoping to spray Caroline with pebbles. But looking in her rear-view mirror she sees she's already gone back inside.

Zandra is in the kitchen anxiously looking at Caroline's face as she enters. She is wiping away tears, ringing her hands in despair. Caroline's expression has transformed from one of venom to one of self-pity. She sobs, 'Oh Zandra, I'm devastated. I don't know what to say or do anymore. I tried apologising to her for everything but she wouldn't listen. I pleaded with her not to go but you know what she's like once she's got the bit between her teeth. That poor, poor sweet girl. I feel so sorry for her. Now she's so alone. How can I make it up to her? There must be *something* I can do.'

Zandra looks her at her directly. Is she telling the truth? It's so hard to tell but she's apologised over and over again for her transgressions against her and the others. She looks sincere. She has to believe her. Give her a chance of redemption. The others definitely had, hadn't they? And Abigail? Well, she's a mess at the moment with everything going on with her. She'll come around eventually. For Zandra now, in front of her is a woman who is desperately sorry and upset and has turned over a new leaf. It's almost a religious transformation. She's so believable. She puts her arms around her and says, 'Don't worry

Caroline. I'll have a word with her tomorrow and I'm sure I can put things right.'

As they hug, Caroline looks at her reflection in the kitchen window and winks at herself.

It's all so very, very easy.

CHAPTER FIVE

Abigail is convulsed with a mixture of rage and betrayal, overridden with a knee-shaking sense of stupidity that she's been blinded for so many years to her husband's constant betrayal with that bitch Caroline, her former best friend. Or was she?

Doubts creep into her mind. Was it even possible? Caroline was living in America most of the time she was married. Was she just saying all that to be nasty? Hadn't she done enough to her on her wedding day? She mentally shrugs the revelation aside. It hardly mattered now, not in the big scheme of things. Baz was gone anyway. Period. She tells herself, *let it go, move on.* For years she'd known he was a lying cheating sod. Caroline's speech has simple underlined the fact and she was well rid of a man like that.

The tiny break in the storm has gone. The weather is getting even worse than before. She now nervously regrets her rashness in leaving the safety and warmth of Zandra's home to battle a storm building in anger.

The rain coupled with the darkness of the night are making it virtually impossible to see. She narrowly misses smacking into a signpost which unexpectedly leaps out front of her, partially lit by a flickering overhead lamp and indicating that she is going in exactly the opposite direction of her house. 'Where's the Goddamn edge of the road?' she shouts with her hands gripping the steering wheel so tightly her knuckles have drained of colour. It's getting harder and harder to navigate the tarmac and *now* she's heading away from her house! 'Why is this happening to me?' she says, tearfully. 'Why me? What did I do to deserve *any* of this? Where's Karma when you need it?'

Without considering any consequences she slams both feet on her brakes, the car slewing to the right and left, and suddenly her rear-view mirror is full of rapidly approaching headlights, accompanied by angry blasts of the horn from the driver behind. She sits paralysed waiting for the inevitable impact as she watches the car behind aquaplane towards her. She feels dizzy until she realises she's been holding her breath. She sends a silent prayer upwards. He's managed to avoid the crunch. She sits there impatiently waiting for the man to overtake her and drive on.

As she waits, the noise of the rain on the roof and the sound of the windscreen wipers backwards and forwards, backward and forwards, scraping the torrent away resonates loudly in the car. It seems like an eternity that both cars are stationery. What is he waiting for, a gold-plated invitation? She looks at him in her rear-view mirror and waves her hand at him impatiently to move on.

Reluctantly she winds down the window sticking her arm out and frantically signals for him to overtake. The coldness of the storm invades the car, taking her by surprise. She winds it back up rapidly, cursing. She is now soaking wet through for the second time tonight. And *still,* he's not moving off. 'Half-wit. Move moron. Cretin,' she shouts, her hand still waving at him manically but now from back inside the car.

The next minute he's there alongside the car and banging on her window motioning for her to wind down the window. She panics, terrified he's going to attack her. Instead of pressing the lock button she winds all the windows down letting the rain back in. He is yelling at her but his face is barely visible in the storm. The wind grabbing at his speech, but she hears him repeat her very words aimed at him previously and now at her bizarrely. 'Are you a moron?' he says. 'What's the matter with you? Have you been drinking? Do you realise you how close you came to killing us both?' And then he says, 'Get out, get out of the car!'

He's going to kill her, she's sure of it. There's nothing for it. She shoves the gear lever into first, flattens her foot down on the accelerator and shoots off, causing the road rage man to fall backwards into the road. He's not going to give up that easily. A minute later the headlights are back in the rear-view mirror. He is tailgating her and seemingly now doesn't care if he's claiming the adjective of being reckless. As much as she puts her foot down, he's there behind her, kissing her bumper. Terrified of what he is going to do her, eyes are darting everywhere for an escape route. A roundabout unexpectedly looming ahead causes her to skid slightly and lose control, although she's more than thankful for fresh options. She breathes a sigh of relief. She'll whizz around a couple of times thinking that'll confuse him.

Her hope is in vain. As she turns the wheel circling the roundabout, he is following her so close to her bumper it's as if he's attached to it. She takes a chance and circles around again but he's still there, like a leech. She's panicking. She's terrified that he's hell-bent on killing her. Murder by road-rage? It's a growing crime now, isn't it? She doesn't know what to do. She's getting dizzy with driving around in circles. Signalling first, she yanks the wheel to the right and turns off desperately hoping she's false footed him. But no, he's still on her tail. She reaches across for her bag on the seat next to her and fumbles inside to find her phone. She has no option. She has to phone for the police and risk them breathalysing her. Better than being run off the road by this monster.

Strangely it is as if the man is telepathic or maybe he is so close he can see her hand on the mobile. A second later he unexpectedly backs off. She continually glances in the rear-view mirror, relieved to see his headlights are getting smaller and smaller. 'What a complete nutter,' she says relaxing slightly, 'total idiot.' She continues along the road constantly checking in her mirror, fearful he'll reappear. After a couple of minutes, she's almost satisfied that maybe he's had enough of the cat-and-mouse game. Perhaps it scared the hell out of him as much as it did her.

The reprieve rather than making her feel better has drained her. That and the row with Caroline has turned her into a physical wreck. Abigail ponders for a moment as to whether she should park up and get her equilibrium back. The worry is she could be a sitting target for another driver to smash into, bearing in mind the visibility is now even worse. There is no choice. She must keep going. She switches on the radio and takes deep breaths to calm herself down. But the static from the thunderstorm is too much. She switches to the CD player. She presses the reject button on the steering column on tune after tune as each one immediately brings tears to her eyes thinking about happier times with Baz. Maybe there's another CD in the dash she wonders.

She hunts for a new CD and takes her eyes off the road for a split second, she is sure that is all it was. A fox is standing in the middle of the road mesmerised by the headlights. Its eyes are an iridescent bright green, eerily so. As they stare into each other's eyes, or so it seems, for that very split second, her immediate instinct is to spin the wheel hard right to avoid the impact before she considers the consequences of that impetuous action.

Abigail's life does not flash before her as she had imagined it would in her musings or nightmares. She does not scream. Her hands forcefully grip the wheel bizarrely convinced this round circle of metal and plastic might save her life as the car turns over. And over. And over. And over.

Her last memory is of the fox still standing there. Still watching. But she can't see anything now. The fox slowly lopes away, totally unscathed.

CHAPTER SIX

Victoria is in the kitchen putting things in the dishwasher. Saoirse is helping her. 'For two pins I would have jumped in the car with her you know,' she says. 'I'm not that happy staying here now, are you?' She whispers, 'I think Caroline is a total bitch. In fact, I *know* she's a total bitch. What do you think about her?'

'Let's say I've known better Friday nights.' Saoirse pauses, 'Why exactly did Abby and Caroline fall out all those years ago, do you know?'

Victoria checks no-one's nearby and answers softly, 'I'm not positive because Abby point-blank refuses to talk about it, *ever*— says it's too upsetting. And Zandra, well, you know Zandra, head in the clouds, Confession *every* Sunday, if not more. Never believes ill of anyone. Mrs Nice-Guy.' She leans forward, 'Word was Baz and Caroline were going at it full pelt on Abby's wedding day.'

Saoirse pulls a face, 'Yeah, that's what I heard too, only I was hoping the rumour machine had got it wrong. Who does that? What a cow and what a bastard Basil is. Never liked him. His eyes were too squinty for my liking. What beats me is that Abby stayed with him for so long.'

'Me too.' Victoria's eyes widen. She gives a slight nod to the right. Someone's coming.

It's Caroline.

'Hello you two. Oh goodness, you've left nothing for me to do. You've done it all and I was just on my way to help.'

'Well, you're too late.'

'I'll put the kettle on then, shall I? Should I make some bedtime cocoa?'

Saoirse says sarcastically, 'Oh, so we're being sent to bed early now, are we? Why's that? Did we do something wrong?'

'Of course not. This isn't my house, I'm not in charge,' she simpers.

Victoria mutters, 'Well you're acting like you are.'

Caroline's eyes fill with tears and she wipes them away with her hands which she then waves underneath as if to calm herself down. 'I know what you all think of me,' she says, sniffing, 'and what I've done in the past but truly I've turned over a new leaf. I'm a different person to who I was twenty years ago. You only have to ask my friends in the US, they'll tell you. If there's anyone in trouble, I'm there, straight away.'

Victoria cannot resist saying almost inaudibly, 'I bet you are.'

If Caroline has heard she doesn't respond to the comment but continues to justify herself. 'You know even though she'll deny it, I must tell you I can't remember the amount of times I've contacted Abigail over the years to apologise. I've simply lost track. I've constantly been trying to make it up to her but you know Abigail, stubborn as a mule. Everything set in stone with her. Once she's made up her mind there's no dissuading her otherwise. I've sent emails, texts, presents even, but she refuses to listen to any explanations. You don't know her like I do. She's *very* bull-headed. Upsetting really.' She wipes a tear, takes a breath. 'She relishes in holding a grudge and there's nothing anyone can do with someone like that. It's very distressing and incredibly hurtful, you know? I honestly don't think I deserve the trauma she always directs at me,' she says, her chest beginning to heave as if she's trying to hold down the tears.

'Oh, there you all are, I was beginning to think you'd *all* gone home—,' Zandra stops mid-sentence. She looks at Caroline's face and then the others. 'Goodness gracious me, what *is* going on here? Caroline?'

She's snivelling, still, chest heaving. She turns to go and says over her shoulder, 'It's nothing, Zandra, please don't concern yourself. I'm fine.'

Zandra asks firmly, 'What exactly *have* you two been saying to her? Why is Caroline so upset?' She runs after her into the living room where they can hear her openly and loudly sobbing her heart out, and Zandra is comforting her.

'What do you think?' Saoirse asks, 'Have we got it all wrong? Are we being too judgemental? Maybe everything she did when we were kids wasn't intentional. Maybe she was going through some stuff we didn't know about.'

'And took it out on us? Did you do that? Ever?'

Saoirse shakes her head slowly, 'Don't think so. Well—I guess maybe I did with my parents, but doesn't everyone do that? It's what you're supposed to do, right? Your true purpose as a kid. I don't recall being bitchy to you lot. Was I?'

Victoria looks pensive, and doesn't answer immediately.

'Goodness, well that's not very good if you had to think about it. Maybe I have been. I can't say I've lived a perfect life, can you?'

Victoria answers, 'Don't be nuts. Yeah, course I don't remember you being nasty, not ever. Anyway, no-one's perfect but that's not the point.'

Saoirse grins, 'Except for me. Didn't you know that I'm perfect?' she jokes. Saoirse combs her long hair with her fingers dragging it back and then tying it in a knot at the back of her head. She says, thoughtfully, 'Oh God I hate saying this but I suppose everyone deserves more than one chance in their lives. Should we be giving her credit for apologising?'

Victoria leans against the worktop and folds her arms looking downwards at her feet. She looks up suddenly, 'It would be nice to know what her friends in America think of her before making a final judgement, wouldn't it? But I suppose that's never going to happen.'

'Yeah, if she's *got* any friends, what do you think?'

'Dunno. Guess it's difficult to live a couple of decades without making friends somewhere along the line, whatever country you're living in.'

'So, what are you saying? Man-up and befriend the bitch?'

This time Victoria does laugh out loud, 'Nicely put.'

CHAPTER SEVEN

'What do you mean by an induced coma? Does that mean Mum's brain is damaged?' sobs Hannah, ringing her hands in despair. Zandra has her arm around the trembling girl trying to comfort her through her own tears.

The ICU doctor is in green scrubs. He's a good-looking man of about twenty-five, far too young, Zandra thinks, to be in charge of her best friend as she lies nearby in a hospital bed. She looks around hoping to see someone with older bones and more experience.

'No, it doesn't mean that at all. Basically, because of the head trauma we've put her into an induced coma to help with any swelling of the brain.'

'Swelling of the brain?' Hannah screams in horror, 'That's terrible. How long will she be like that? Months? Years? Until you think she's been on the machine too long because it costs the NHS too much? And then you'll switch her off?' Her fists are clenched by her side as she demands defiantly, 'I need to talk to my Mum to see if she's all right.' Hannah won't let up. She's taken the break-up of her parents badly, even though she's internalised her feelings so much that neither of them has realised it. The thought she will lose her mother completely, or that her life will be less than it was, is the final straw for the teenager.

The ICU doctor is not handling things well. He's getting flustered. 'You really need to calm down. Your attitude is not going to help your mother get better any quicker. I cannot be specific. All I can say is that hopefully it will not be for long and she'll be fine afterwards.'

Hannah stands her ground. 'I want guarantees and if you won't give them to me then I want to speak with someone who will. Who's in charge here? I want to speak to the head doctor.'

The doctor sighs. He's used to this. It's hard dealing with patients who have horrendous injuries but that's his job. He accepts that some days will be better than others. But patients' families are another thing. There was no real advice on developing a bedside manner in his medical curriculum that he can recall, or if there was, he must have been off sick with a hangover that day.

He turns and grabs a passing nurse and asks, 'Any chance you could take these good people to the family room and calm them down?'

Hannah shouts, 'I am calm. I am very calm. I just want to know if—I mean, when, I can speak with my mother? What's the problem with that?'

Zandra looks embarrassed. 'Sorry,' she says, 'she's a bit upset, she's not normally like this.'

'Auntie Zandra,' Hannah says, really quite annoyed now, 'how do you know what I'm *normally* like and what does it matter anyway? *Normally,* I have *two* parents. *Normally,* I am at home playing music, or hanging out with my friends. *Normally,* I'm not in some dumb hospital desperately worried about my Mum, *normally* not wondering if she's about to die.'

The doctor mutters something under his breath.

'What did you say?' Hannah snaps. 'Did you just call me a drama queen?'

The young man's complexion turns bright red. The nurse takes Hannah's arm gently, 'Come on love, let's get you a nice cup of tea and have a chat.'

Meekly she allows the nurse to take her away from the ICU into the family room.

As she does so, another nurse says to the young doctor, 'I don't envy you her.'

'Sometimes Nurse Coolidge, I hate my job.'

'Only sometimes?' asks the nurse, laughing.

***

Abigail had been in the ICU a good twenty-four hours before Hannah knew anything about it, not that the hospital hadn't tried to track her down. She'd been partying at another friend's house whose parents were aware for the night. Pretty much every kid in a forty-mile area had turned up. There was too much booze and reefers aplenty. Panic hit the revelry when somebody shouted that the police were outside which caused mayhem; a mad rush to shove the weed down the toilet and avoid being busted. It was a false alarm. It was the countryside and instead of the police arriving, it was a family of angry geese who had got a bit snippy with one of the boys who was having a pee outside by the large pond.

The party rebooted once the panic subsided and by 1am the neighbours had had enough of puking teenagers and open toileting. More and more people kept turning up. It had got out of control and by 2am the throng had spilled over into the road and the music was throbbing the walls of neighbouring houses.

This time it was the police and not the geese but no-one dumped their drugs thinking it was all one big joke. The police cleared out the mob and cherry-picked a few kids to wheel down to the station for a talking to and one of those kids happened to be Hannah.

While her mother was being wheeled into Intensive Care after an operation, Hannah was hauled up in the police station and subjected to a severe dressing down. She was told to call her mother. She prayed she wouldn't answer. She didn't of course and were it not for a kinder policeman, her phone would have gone to voicemail had he not picked it up.

'Is there someone with you, an adult, or anyone I can talk to, Hannah?' she asked.

'Why what's wrong?' said Hannah, sensing alarm. 'Is it my mum? Is she OK? What's going on? Why are you calling from her phone?'

The policeman hearing the concern in Hannah's voice, took the phone from her. 'Who is this please?' she asked.

'Well as I made the call, perhaps you could tell me who you are?' said the woman.

'I am PC Smithers. Hannah is at the station answering questions about her participation in an illegal rave.'

There was another pause, and the female voice answered, 'Right, OK, sorry to hear that. This is Mrs Hamley. I'm a medical social worker and I've been asked to contact Hannah as her mother Abigail is in intensive care. She was in a rather nasty road accident.'

'Is it serious?'

'We hope not but I do feel it's best if Hannah is close by at her mother's side for obvious reasons.' Hannah was driven down to the hospital and arrived looking very sorry for herself. Two hours later, Zandra was at her side.

CHAPTER EIGHT

A month before, Florida.
The man awakes, his eyes tight shut. He stretches, then gives his genitalia a thorough scratch, yawning as he does so. Then, sliding his feet off the bed onto the ground, his hands pressed into the soft mattress, he stands up, his arms above his head. He drops them by his side and glances over at the naked woman still lying fast asleep on the bed, her ample rump rounded and exposed to the daylight. He thinks how tempting it is to give it a hearty slap, but he knows that will induce a rage which might not be followed by an invitation to come back to bed.

Instead, he pads over to the floor length windows, his feet sinking into the lush carpet. He quietly slides open the window and steps out onto the balcony of the condo. The heat of the morning hits him in his face, together with the noise and pollution from the street below. It takes his breath away. The hubbub of cars, people, sirens, overhead jets flying to and from faraway destinations for a brief moment causes him inexplicable pain. Something in his brain has triggered a bad memory. He shoves the thought to one side and looks back into the room at the sleeping naked female and smiles. How easy it has been. But then *she* was easy. He considers scornfully how *she* regards herself as the con artist. How pathetic for her to believe he could be taken in by her deceit. Although underlying her fake vulnerability and coquettishness, her lies, her schemes, weirdly he could tell she was a needy female, desperate to feel wanted emotionally and sexually. She was still an attractive woman in spite of, rather than because of, obvious attempts at recapturing her youthful looks. Botox had not been her friend. The man sighs wondering why so many females attempt to rid themselves of the roundness of their bodies preferring their clothes to hang straight down instead of moulding to their shape.

The blonde stirs slightly, reaches out her hand to feel the vacant spot where the man had been, turns over, revealing her naked breasts, lifts her head up and looks at him. 'Come back to bed,' she says, 'You've unfinished business.' She smiles at him and says, 'Unless of course you can't manage it.' Using every part of her sensuality and nakedness she slowly sits up, her knees tucked under her chin, her arms hugging her crossed legs modestly hiding herself, her mouth adopting a pout as she beckons him over.

Emmett Ryder glances at his watch. He is due to send in a report within the hour. He does a quick calculation in his head as he watches her, realising one part of his body is way ahead of him in the computation and thinks to himself, *Why not?*
As their bodies rhythmically move towards each

other's climax, Emmett wonders how many more times this will be happening before Caroline is wearing an orange uniform with chains around her ankles.

CHAPTER NINE

Abigail is finding it hard to open her eyes. They feel like they've been glued shut. Slowly but slowly, she manages to force them open. She winces in pain as she blinks at the bright lights shining all around her, confused as to where she is. Had she fallen asleep downstairs? Weirdly she can hear a series of bleeps and a hubbub of people talking quietly, the squeak of soft shoes, metal on metal. The pain in her head is killing her and she can't turn it very easily; something seems to be preventing it. She tries to lift up her hand but something is weighing it down. As she pulls it towards her face, she is shocked to see wires attached to it. Then it comes flooding back to her. The accident. Instantly her stomach turns and she feels nauseous as she remembers the fox; its eyes staring at her in the middle of the street; the rain sheeting down on her windscreen; the wipers manically trying to give her a clear vision of the road; her desperation in avoiding the animal standing there, mesmerised and unable to move; and then the car turning over and over and over, as she desperately tried to hang onto the steering wheel. The jerk of the G-force as her body was face-up one minute and then down the next. The sickening final turn as the car seemed to be balancing on its side for what seemed a lifetime, her body weighted heavily against the door and then the shuddering crash as it righted itself, the movement reverberating through her body causing a rippling wave of agonising pain.

She struggles to remember what came next. There is a ghostly recollection of someone asking her if she is all right and her answering that *she thinks so*. That though seems to be the last thing she can recall. Until now. She figures she must be in a hospital. Which one?

'Oh good, you're awake finally,' says a smiling nurse. 'Fancy a cuppa?'

Abby licks her lips, they're very dry. 'Am I allowed?' she asks.

The nurse beams. 'Of course, you're allowed. Only sips mind. And you can have a piece of toast if you behave yourself.'

'How did I get here?' she asks, struggling to shift herself into a sitting position on the bed. 'Sorry, that was a bit dumb, in an ambulance I guess.' The effort to move is proving difficult, particularly as the pain is intense. Abigail asks tentatively, fighting back the emotion and worry, 'Am I badly hurt?'

'Hang on, I'll help you.' The nurse helps her to sit up, plumping the pillows, then she puts a thermometer in her mouth. 'Don't try to talk,' she says, checking her pulse, noting statistics from the automatic blood pressure machine. 'How about if I get Doctor Green to have a word? OK?'

Abigail mumbles, the thermometer still in her mouth. 'Sorry, hang on,' the nurse says taking it out. 'What did you say?'

'Hannah, my daughter, does she know I'm here? Is she OK?' Abigail tries to recall with difficulty if Hannah was with her in the car. She can't remember. Everything is disjointed. Muddled up.

'Your daughter? Oh yes, no worries. Hannah's fine. She'll be here soon. She usually comes about now, with her aunt.'

'Aunt?'

'Yes, tall thin lady with red hair.'

'Zandra?'

'That's right. Sorry Abby, it is Abby isn't it, or do you prefer Abigail?'

'Abby's fine.'

'Couldn't tell you her name. All I know is only relatives are allowed and she said she was your sister, if that's—'

'No, no, sorry, sorry. Yes, she's my sister. Don't know what's the matter with me. Bit concussed I guess.'

'Yes, you are,' answers the nurse dubiously aware of all the other so-called relatives who have never been relatives coming to visit. Trouble is she thinks the relatives who should visit mostly don't, or if they do, their first question is usually, 'How many days has he or she got left?' Ghouls, some of them. The thoughts don't please her and she wonders to herself that a shop job might have been less stressful, at least it wouldn't be keeping her awake at night.

When the three females catch sight of each other it's hard to say who's crying the most.

'Oh Mum, what did you do? And why were you going the wrong way? Where were you driving to? Why did you go out in that terrible storm? Was it because of me? Why—'

Zandra stops her. 'Goodness Hannah, too many questions. Give your poor Mum a chance to get her breath back.' She pauses, 'Actually, Abby, why *were* you going in the wrong direction.'

Abby shakes her head and then out of the blue she remembers slamming on the brakes and the tailgating maniac behind her. In the end she wasn't sure *where* she was going.

'Could we talk about this another time please?'

'Of course, of course.' Zandra pats her arm. 'How are you feeling though? Are they being nice to you in here?'

Abby grins. Zandra sometimes reminds her of her mother. 'I haven't a clue whether they're being nice to me or not Zandra. I've only been awake less than half an hour. What I need to know is how badly hurt I am. Is there anything I should be worried about?'

Hannah's face is white with anxiety as she answers, 'They think you're OK. You've had a couple of scans on your back and it all seems to be all right.'

'Seems to be?'

'Well, it's just they can't tell for sure until you're well enough to get on your feet.'

Abby pulls herself up and tries to swing her legs over the bed, causing one of the wires to wobble a little and the machine to bleep madly, 'OK so why don't we put everyone's mind at rest and see now, shall we?'

A nurse and a young doctor come bounding up, 'What's going on here?'

Abby stares at the doctor defiantly, 'I need to get up to go to the toilet,' she demands.

'There's no need for that love,' says the nurse, and points to a bag below the bed. 'Catheter', she mouths.

Abby can now feel the tug of it, annoyingly. 'Right,' she suggests, 'Why don't we ditch that and see if I can make my own way to the facility, if that's all right by you?'

The doctor is uncertain. He's new to the ICU. 'I think we'll leave it until Mr Braithwaite comes, if you don't mind. He's your consultant surgeon.'

'Surgeon? Did I have an operation? What for?'

The nurse and doctor exchange looks, the doctor desperate for the nurse to jump in and rescue him. Reluctantly the older of the two takes charge. She begins to straighten the sheets, tucking them in tight into the bed and pulling Abby forward so she can re-plump the pillows. 'Mr Braithwaite will explain everything. He's due in about an hour. Meantime I think you'd better settle down for a bit. Sorry ladies, but Abby needs her rest. All this excitement isn't helping her blood pressure. Off you go now.'

'But we've only just come.'

'Well OK then, twenty minutes max.'

Begrudgingly twenty minutes later Hannah and Zandra do as they're told. Hannah walks backwards, hanging onto Zandra for support, constantly waving and blowing her mother kisses, mouthing, 'Love you Mum, love you,' interlaced with, 'Sorry Mum, sorry.' Abby blows the kisses back with the hand free of encumbrances and attempts to hold down the panic that is building inside her. What have they removed from	her	body?

CHAPTER TEN

Victoria is trying in vain to speak to Gwen but her phone is ringing out. She's a grandmother now and is dangling one child off her skirt while the other is clinging to her hip. Being a grandmother is not quite what she had thought it would be. She's exhausted. The child closest to her ear is screaming for a biscuit and the other, now, is trying to grab the phone that's ringing but is actually pushing it out of reach of Gwen's hand. It's all very trying.

'Hello,' she says, quite breathy. She sounds worn out.

'It's me,' says Victoria.

'Who?'

'It's me, Gwen.'

'Who's me?'

'Victoria.'

'Oh!' she says. 'Do you realise, saying *it's me* is not helpful when everyone says, *oh it's me*!

'Aren't I in your phone, my number I mean?'

'Well, yes but I didn't look. Got two very energetic children pulling my arms off,' she tells her as she hands the entire packet of biscuits to the two kids, conceding defeat. *What the hell, I'm just the granny, not the mother, let them eat what the hell they want.*

Victoria laughs. 'You never change Gwen that's why I love you,' she pauses, 'only in a friendship way of course.' Victoria, having hidden her sexuality for so many heart-breaking years until recently is still anxious the world should understand exactly what side of the sexual spectrum she sits. Any time that word *love* is mentioned, she's desperate for it to be instantly quantified.

'Victoria darling, or as I now know you prefer, Vic, I am a mother of five, a grandmother of three point two children, and although I am firmly ensconced in feminism and all it stands for, I also practice my feminism to the extent I have never succumbed to wearing trousers or indeed pyjama bottoms. Have no fear Vic you can say you love me to your heart's content and I will not bat one blue-shadowed eyelid.'

Victoria laughs again, 'Still using blue? Be brave, live a little, try green. However, my reason for ringing is not exactly a happy one.'

'Oh, what's happened?'

'I tried to ring you a couple of days ago.'

'Yes, sorry I should have rung back. We were all up in Scotland, hired a croft up there. Very remote and absolutely no internet. Total bliss.'

'Sounds it.' She pauses again. 'It's Abigail. She crashed her car.'

Victoria hears Gwen gasp, and rushes on, 'Don't worry, she's OK. She's in hospital, but according to Zandra it wasn't exactly straight forward. They had to remove her spleen apparently. Obviously, that's not the greatest outcome and of course now she's susceptible to any infection going, but that's life, isn't it? Problem is, the hospital is in special measures because they've been under attack from some viral bug for the past three months.'

Gwen holds onto the work surface to steady herself. Out of all the girls, Abigail has always been her favourite. When the six girls first met and formed their group all those years ago at school, Gwen had hoped Abigail would be her *special* friend. She'd been heartbroken that Abigail had chosen Caroline instead. They were inseparable. The eleven-year-old Gwen had taken an instant dislike to Caroline. She'd been bullied at her primary school and saw all the signs of the same character defect in Caroline. But Caroline was more of a controller than a bully. She manipulated people. She would set social traps for people, stirring up trouble, dropping false accusations into the melting pot and then sit back enjoying the ensuing melee of anger and distrust, and always, always, when it seemed the finger might point in her direction, burst into tears, appealing for unfounded sympathy.

In essence, Gwen had never liked her and in her mind never would. Because of the others she only ever tolerated her as one of the group. Instantly she asks Victoria, 'I take it this crash happened the evening of the Grand Reunion and Caroline was most likely the instigator?'

Victoria hesitates, 'Yes and no. Abbs did flip out that night. She said she couldn't stomach the fact we'd all forgiven Caroline for everything she'd done to us over the years.'

'And have you?'

'I don't know.'

'I blame myself for this,' says Gwen. 'If I'd been there maybe she wouldn't have gone out in the storm and—'

'Don't be nuts Gwen. Abbs wasn't prepared to listen to anyone that night, believe me, she had an agenda.'

'So, I ask again. Have you forgiven Caroline for everything?'

Victoria hesitates a moments and replies, 'The problem is Gwen, I've had a lifetime of angst in not admitting who I am, and I've had enough of black clouds hanging over my head to last two lifetimes. Yeah, Caroline was a right bitch to me and if I'm honest it was her actions and her constant jibes which almost tipped me over the edge. My family were in pieces. Do you know even now, at times, I can see the look in their eyes wondering if I'm going to try and do something stupid again when my life takes a downward turn and this time not mix up the bottles of pills.' She does a nervous laugh.

'If you want to know what I think,' Victoria continues, 'like I said, Abigail had an agenda that night. I reckon she was determined not to accept any apology Caroline was prepared to offer, if she was going to apologise that is. I'm positive she was only there for a chance to say her piece. She'd held back for all those years internalising and something had to give. But to rush out into that awful storm, it just shows how angry she's been and she was very angry. She's normally so rational but you know Caroline, she can get right under your skin. It was literally an accident waiting to happen. And then it did.'

Gwen wipes the mist that is building in her eyes as she tries not to cry. 'If anything happens to Abigail,' she says, 'I won't be able to forgive her regardless of any explanation or apology. She's a dreadful woman even though she did nothing to me of course,' she adds in afterthought.

'You say we shouldn't give her a second chance but surely we have to give people the space to change their ways, don't we? Even the hardest criminal can repent.'

Gwen snorts. 'I never realised you would be such an easy target for her false promises. Besides it's not important. What I need to know now is when can I go and visit dear Abby and where?'

Victoria is rankled by Gwen's aspersion to her naivety in giving into Caroline. She replies shortly, 'No visitors presently, only family. Oh, and before you ask, no flowers or cards either.'

Gwen bristles slightly at Victoria's sudden coldness and says equally icily, 'Well it was good of you to phone. I'd be grateful if you would keep me advised of further developments.'

Victoria is taken aback at the change of tone and responds accordingly, 'Will do. Bye then.'

'Bye.'

Both women stare at their cells, equally annoyed with themselves, knowing it's not each other they're suddenly angry with, but Caroline.

Gwen relents first and rings back praying that Victoria won't have taken umbrage and will pick up the phone.

'Yes.'

'Victoria, Vic, darling. I'm sorry. Don't let's fall out especially over Caroline. You're right, it's the

Christian thing to do. I'll try and think positively about her.'

Victoria says sorrowfully, 'Gwen, I'm sorry too. I shouldn't be such an arsehole. You're right to be suspicious and maybe I've been too quick to accept her change of heart. After all, when has she not been a manipulating toad?'

They both laugh. Gwen says, 'It's almost like being back at school isn't it, squabbling over the silly woman? By the way where's Hannah staying? Remember there's always room for her here, one more wouldn't make a bit of difference to me and in fact she could be quite useful with the twins.'

'You're out of luck love, she's with Zandra, and apart from worrying about her Mum, Zandra is spoiling her rotten, so it's not all bad.'

'With Caroline there?'

'No, not at the moment, thankfully. She's allegedly visiting a friend in London.' Then she adds, 'Let's hope she stays there. Permanently.'

'Couldn't have put it better myself.'

CHAPTER ELEVEN

That morning Emmett Ryder has studied the contents of his hold-all. Should he wear a suit or dress down completely? In the end he settles for a white Oxford button-down, washed-out blue Levi's, completed by a pale blue cotton jacket, feeling a casual smart look is the best solution. He studies himself in the mirror, rubs his chin and decides maybe the designer stubble is too much. As he shaves, he rehearses his speech, wondering if this is the right thing to do? Will it end with the UK police knocking at his hotel room door? He has to take the chance.

Two hours later he is outside the hospital still debating if he's doing the right thing? He's a ballsy guy, at least he thinks he is. Automatically he does his usual routine of checking he has his cell, his wallet, his ID, and then last of all he pats his chest where his Colt usually resides, remembering suddenly its absence. He feels naked without it, and curses the strict UK gun laws. He mutters to himself, 'Backward sons of bitches, why don't they join the real world?'

Emmett stands in front of the hospital *menu* of departments, his eyes scanning up and down until an ancient looking man, his gnarled hands bloodless as he tightly grips his crutches, nudges him in the arm with his elbow, 'Nightmare innit?'

''Scuse me?'

The ancient head nods towards the noticeboard. 'Nightmare trying to find out where to go. Reckon if you were about to breathe your last breath, you'd be dead before you got there. Then the bastards think it's helpful to paint coloured lines on the floor. Who do they think we are, the cast of the Wizard of Oz?'

'Quite.' Emmett tries to escape, but his new companion is thrilled that at last someone is listening to his moans.

'Tell me where you want to go mate. I know this hospital like the back of my hand, I've been here so many times. I've had a gall bladder removed, in-growing toenail, dodgy prostrate, wisdom teeth— all out.' At that he pulls open his mouth with the wrinkled fingers of one hand, revealing a yellow furry looking tongue hovering over blackened stumps. 'That was something else, that was. God the pain. And the swelling! Looked like I had cricket balls in my gob. Both sides. Then I broke my leg in the winter of '96, or was it '97? Tell a lie, it was neither, it was 2000. The millennium. And I tell you why I particularly remember, it was because we were all petrified the computers were going to crash, and I was rigged up to—'

Emmett holds up his hand, 'Man, I have to stop you there. I'm in a bit of a rush. See the woman,' he falters, 'I mean, my cousin, is desperately ill in ICU.' He blows his cheeks out dramatically and pretends to wipe a tear from his eye. 'Who knows if I'll be in time.'

The old man shakes his head knowingly and balancing on one crutch takes his wizened hand out of the other and clutches at Emmett's sleeve, and sounding as if he has a lump in his throat says, 'You go, old son, you go.' And then he adds, his voice totally normal again, 'It's down that corridor on the left, take first right and then it's straight on. OK? Got that?'

Emmett pulls away from the man mumbling his thanks. He looks down at his light-coloured jacket and notices dark finger marks where his jacket was grabbed by the ancient one's greasy hand. He swears under his breath, follows the directions given and finds himself outside the ICU alongside a couple hanging around, the girl red-eyed and distraught while her male companion has a totally disinterested air. People he thinks. Some you hate. Others you hate more.

Then briefly worried they might be visiting Abigail also, he says, 'Terrible times, eh?'

The male looks at him directly, 'Yeah. Who you here for?'

'My, er, my cousin, Abigail Davidson. How about you?'

He inclines his head towards the girl. 'Her grandfather.' He leans over and adds, 'It'll be a relief for all of us when he croaks, the miserable old bastard. And it'll save all the money that's coming out of our inheritance on his nursing home fees. Frightening they are. Talk about arm and a leg. And what for? So he can be miserable and make us even more miserable when we're forced to visit the old sod.'

Emmett is not surprised. He's used to callousness. He lives and breathes it. He agrees, 'Right, right, yeah, know what you mean.'

Luckily before the conversation can take an even more downward turn, the ICU door clicks, indicating the lock has been released. The threesome walk in and don the plastic garments provided. He asks a nurse, 'Looking for Abigail Davidson, could you direct me please?'

She looks at him suspiciously, 'You've not been here before, have you?'

'Er, no ma'am, no I haven't. Just flown in from the States especially to see her.'

'You're American?'

'Yes ma'am, I'm American. I'm her Cousin Emmett from the mid-West.' He decides not to lie about his name in case he's pressed for ID.

'Were you expected? It's just no-one mentioned she had an American cousin? It's usually only her daughter and sister.'

He thinks to himself, *Does everyone get the third degree around here?* 'No, it's a surprise.'

Begrudgingly she says, 'End of the room on the right, and don't tire her out. Remember, she might be awake but she's still very poorly.' As he's walking away she calls after him, 'Did you want to talk to the doctor?'

His eyes widen, 'No ma'am, no that's fine.'

'Mm. OK, but remember, don't—'

'Yeah, I know, don't tire her out. Got it,' and he tips an imaginary hat.

Abigail is sitting up in bed dozing. He takes the chance to study her face and is surprised to find she's quite attractive and not as he had imagined. He needs to talk to her urgently and before any other visitors arrive, namely her daughter and her sister which will blow his cover completely. So, he puts his hand on her arm and gently shakes it, saying, 'Abigail. Um, Abby?' he tries.

She breathes deeply and shifts her arm slightly. He repeats the action and she takes her other arm, complete with its attaching wires, and attempts to brush off what's annoying her when she suddenly realises it's actually a person. Her eyes open expecting to find Hannah or a nurse and sees instead a stranger.

Abigail starts, surprised, and then there is a flash of recognition. It dawns on Emmett she is about to scream and without looking around to check, puts his hand over her mouth and warns, 'Don't scream, there's no need to scream, I haven't come here to hurt you. Truly.'

Abigail tries to shrink away from him, pushing back hard into the pillows. He tentatively moves his hand from her mouth saying, 'Sorry I had to do that.'

She glances at her heart rate on the monitor wondering if one of the nurses or doctors might suddenly appear. He notices the look and orders, 'You seriously need to calm down, I'm not your enemy.'

'If you're not my enemy, why did you try to run me off the road, you, you sodding maniac. If it wasn't for you, I wouldn't be here.'

He looks embarrassed. This is not a normal feeling for Emmett, and for once he is speechless. Looking down at her in the bed he says, 'Look I'm sorry if that's the case, obviously I never meant for any of that to happen.' And then he adds, looking confused and rubbing his chin, 'Hold on there I don't actually recall seeing you driving off the road in front of me because if you had I sure as hell would have stopped.'

Abigail's cheeks flush, annoyed with his inference that he had nothing to do with the accident. 'Whatever. Well maybe you weren't actually involved in the crash itself but basically you were the cause. You and your manic driving. Who drives like that in those conditions? So yes, I do blame you—and you and—and—,' she pauses not wanting to mention the wayward fox, and then continues, flustered, 'Well it did happen, and I haven't a clue when I'll be out of here and back to normal, always supposing I can be normal.' She wags her finger at him. 'They took my spleen out. Do you know what that means?'

He shakes his head, 'Er, no ma'am, not really. What's a spleen?'

'I have no idea, but apparently it's very important.'

They stare at each other. Abigail asks him again, 'Who are you? Why were you following me that night? And what the hell are you doing here? Finishing off the job you started? Are you trying to kill me?'

Emmett puts his hands up, 'One thing at a time, please. Yes, I was following you,' and then he lies, 'but only because I was trying to let you know your rear lights weren't working. And then you braked so hard I almost went into the back of you.'

Abigail tries to fold her arms with great difficulty, giving up when the wire to her hand gets in the way. Now, even more annoyed, she says, 'Really? And that's why you banged on the window and began shouting at me, was it? I don't recall hearing any words like *rear* or *lights*. All can remember is a stream of abuse I won't repeat here in case the kindly folks think that's the sort of language I use.'

Emmett has to grin and rubs his chin, 'You got me there. That is true. What can I say?'

'What can you say? Tell me *exactly* what the f—' she stops herself and continues, 'What was the real reason for following me? Simple question deserves a simple answer. That is before I do start screaming or buzzing for the nurse to get you, an imposter, thrown out of here on your arse.'

'Arse? OK. Is that an acceptable word for a young lady to be saying in the hallows of the ICU?' he quips. Then seeing that Abigail is about to explode holds up his hands. 'That was a joke.' He pauses briefly. 'OK, I'll come clean. Yes, I was following you, and yeah, your brake lights were working quite well.'

She interrupts, 'And?'

He waves his hands at her, 'Patience, please. I heard the shouting match with your friend Caroline—'

Abigail barks, 'She is *not* my friend. She *was* my friend, and then she *wasn't.'* Then the words sink in. She looks at him confused, 'Hang on a minute, hang on a minute. This doesn't make any sense. You *heard* the shouting match? You *heard* the shouting match? How the hell could you *hear* a shouting match if you were—'

'Look honey, I don't know if it's the drugs you're taking, but if you keep interrupting me, you'll never find anything out. Please,' and he holds up his hands once more, 'Give me a break.' He takes a deep breath worried at what Abigail's reaction will be to the statement. 'Caroline is a crook, a confidence trickster. I'm an investigator, a US government investigator. The woman's a fraudster. She's been running, or ran a Ponzi scheme in America and all across the planet. I was about to make the arrest in Florida. Then that very morning she'd skipped to Brazil. I tracked her down, even got the extradition order, everything. I was moments away from making the arrest again and then what do you know, she's managed to get out of the country on a fake passport.'

Abigail looks astonished. 'Really? Are you kidding me? What Caroline? A confidence trickster? Her? Go on, she's not bright enough to be a crook. Pull the other one, it's got bells on.'

He pulls a face, and shakes his head, and mutters to himself, 'How did I know this was going to be one of those days? Look ma'am, I wish I was kidding you. Now she's back on home territory where I believe she will do it all over again, and probably with your friends' help; unknowingly of course. Not suggesting you guys are criminals.' He adds when he sees Abigail's expression turn to one of anger yet again.

'Caroline? Are we talking Caroline Smith, that was? You sure you haven't got her mixed up with some other Caroline? Oh, and by the way, please don't keep calling me ma'am, it's Abigail, Abby.'

He grins, 'Abby. Nice name.'

She blushes, 'Thank you.'

'Pleased to meet you.'

'Mm, I'm not sure I can say the same at the moment.'

'Fair comment. Look, as regards Caroline Smith aka Armitage aka Trent aka so many names you wouldn't believe, she is one monster of a bad woman.

She's a pariah. She uses folk mercilessly in order to get contacts for her scams. She's a sociopath and has no remorse or guilt for anything. She'll leech off your friends before they'll even notice their blood has been sucked out.'

Abigail nods. That did sound like the Caroline she used to call a friend. She doesn't want to admit that to this guy, but she's come to that very conclusion herself and years before.

They stare at each other, and then Emmett says, 'Are you starting to believe me?'

'I agree she is a sociopath— good description. She's a nasty piece of work and I despise her, but a crook? A Ponzi scheme? She's not that bright.'

'Well, she is.'

'OK, convince me then, how's she doing it?'

Emmett takes a deep breath, 'Here's the thing. First, it's one whole goddam mess. She gets corrupt builders to slap up a few houses here and there in as many sites as possible so as to make these guys look authentic and successful. The builder gets loans from the parent scam company which then promotes itself as being a good investment, as far as yearly returns are concerned, sucking in all sorts of folks, pensioners, long-term investors, you name it there are gazillions of poor schmucks out there who believe everything they're told, and never check backgrounds. Sometimes, it's simply pure greed. Other times, it's desperation, with folk worried about their future. Other times it's parents saving for their kids' college funds, weddings, funerals even. Meanwhile, the contractor, and I use that word loosely, sells his shit properties over and over again, only getting deposits which are never returned, nothing ever gets sold completely. Mostly nothing ever gets finished so the scam can go on and on and on. Why? Because they need the properties to promote the illusion. And they change the names of the sites to confuse people even more, and all the time bull themselves up as being *the latest thing, award-winning, state-of-the-art,* with ten-year guarantees that aren't worth the paper they're printed on. *If* they ever get printed that is. And it goes without saying they use social media to a merciless extent.'

'So how does Caroline feature in this?'

'Caroline? Oh boy, she's the kingpin, the motherboard, the black widow. She's the enticer. She's the *quote* friendly lady *unquote* who says to the elderly couple in the restaurant, *sorry I overheard you mentioning about investment, I shouldn't be telling you this but*—. She can be *mighty* convincing.'

'I don't get it, if you know all this why hasn't she and the others been stopped so far; sounds pretty simple?'

He puts his head in his hands. 'Out of the mouths of babes—' Emmett looks up, 'Look honey, these guys are scum, but they're expert scum in what they do. They've done it and are doing it over and over and over again. But there's one thing on our side. They are greedy. And dumb. They slip up, and when they do, they sing their heads off. There's no truer saying that there is no loyalty amongst thieves. Forget all the shit in movies about how they don't rat each other out. To save their skins they'd rat each member of their families and future families if they thought it would save them. And they always, always get caught, but it's proving it, getting the 110% proof for the authorities and making it stick. Plus making sure you get every—single—fucking—bastard put behind bars for a long, long time.'

Abigail sits there dumbfounded, not knowing what to say.

'Well, say something.'

She looks puzzled, and scratches her head with the free hand. 'I don't get it. Are you telling me you were out there on Zandra's property skulking around in all that weather? Were you going to arrest her that night?'

'Before we get into all that, firstly I'm truly sorry about the accident. If I helped cause it in any way, believe me that was never my intention.' He looks around and then at his watch, 'When's your daughter due?'

She looks at him, 'Hannah? Oh no, no sweat, don't worry, she's coming tonight.'

'Fine, so we won't be interrupted by family. Here's the thing Abigail, I need your help to nail this bitch, sorry, your friend—'

She reminds him again, 'I keep telling you, she's *not* my friend. She used to be and now she's not. OK? And *I'm* the one who's supposed to be a bit muddled because of the pain-killers! Honestly. As for my,' and she tries to do air quotes with her heads, and then curses after giving up, 'ex-friend, she's a liar, a cheat, and now seemingly, so you tell me, a crook. Well, *there's* a surprise, who would have thought it?'
They look at each other in silence until Abigail says, 'OK, tell me what you want me to do; although how I can do anything when I'm holed up here is rather confusing.   It   had   better   be   some   plan.'

CHAPTER TWELVE

After that fateful, unsuccessful get-together of the old friends, the next morning before any of the others had risen, Caroline had gone. Zandra found a note propped up on an empty Champagne bottle in the kitchen explaining that she had, *Unexpected urgent business. Sorry, and thanks for the hospitality. Be in touch.*

Zandra felt a mixture of relief and annoyance. She'd been relieved Caroline had gone but been quite annoyed that she hadn't had the courtesy to say goodbye in person. How incredibly gauche she thought but then wondered if she had gone for good or if she would come back.

She was not however taken aback to find that Caroline had made no attempt to leave the room as tidy as when it was first offered to her upon her arrival. The duvet was in a heap, discarded on the floor by the window. Magazines were scattered everywhere. A half-empty wine glass sat next to a spent bottle of whisky. The curtains were undrawn and there was no sign of any luggage. She had well and truly gone. The mess annoyed Zandra and instead of waiting for her cleaner, as she usually would have done, she began to straighten the room herself, tugging off the sheets and piling them onto the floor. As she did so she spotted an envelope poking out from under the bed. She hesitated at first. Zandra was raised to respect other people's privacy and not to pry. If a letter was ever delivered by the postman incorrectly at her parents' home it would never have occurred to anyone in Zandra's family to open it *by mistake*. But this was different. If Caroline was definitely not coming back then maybe it was something important that needed to be opened.

Inside the envelope was a photograph of Caroline looking longingly at a tall, good-looking man seated next to her by a swimming pool. On the back she had scrawled, '*Emmett, a memento of that wonderful day, yours Caro xxxxx*'.

As Zandra studied the photograph, she recalled the same man's photo on Caroline's mobile when she was spying. 'Mm, so you *do* have someone important in your life Caroline,' she muttered out loud. 'I knew I was right, even though you gave me the impression you weren't involved with anyone that mattered a jot.'

However, three days later, the room now clean, tidy and back to normal Zandra is both irritated and amazed to find Caroline back on her doorstep, complete with bulging shopping bags, a smiling face, and sickening effusiveness.

'Darling, darling, darling, I'm *b-a-c-k,*' she says in a sing-song way, air-kissing Zandra's both cheeks, which had not been proffered. 'It's only been a couple of days and I've missed you already. Oh, I simply *must* sit down. Goodness shopping is *such* a bore these days. And *so* exhausting. Why does one do it I wonder?'

Zandra corrects her, 'It's been three days actually.' She walks over to the dresser and takes out an envelope and hands it to Caroline, 'I think this is yours. I wasn't snooping but I found it under your bed.'

Caroline takes it and blushes slightly. 'Oh busted! He's um—well, what can I say? Actually you know what, he's no-one. History. A passing ship in a lonely night.'

'It's no business of mine Caroline. It's just I kind of got the distinct impression you didn't have anyone in tow.' And Zandra thinks to herself, *and I wonder what other* impressions *I've been given by you that are skewed?* 'It doesn't matter, your love-life is obviously of no concern to me. I take it you haven't heard about Abigail then?' Zandra says sniffily.

The woman is paying more attention to her purchases than her hostess and says dismissively, 'Abigail, Abigail, Abigail. The drama queen. One of life's victims. Oh, don't tell me, let me guess. She's sold the house? Or found a new man? Is that it? I'd forgotten how tiresome she is with her bleating and constant troubles.' She holds her forehead her eyes closed, 'Really, Zandra sweetie, can we *not* talk about Abigail for a smidgeon, I was in *such* a good mood, shame to spoil it. It's giving me a headache. Oh, and don't put the kettle on, look in one of the bags, I've brought some Bolly for us both, thought we could do with it. And there's some sushi somewhere, next to the cashmere, I think. Are you OK with sushi? I know some people can't abide the thought of eating raw fish.'

Her request is ignored as Zandra says, 'Actually it's nothing as mundane as your rather insulting suggestions. Abigail is in hospital. In intensive care.'

'Oh. Right.' She leans over and whispers even those no-one seems to be close by enough to hear her, 'She didn't decide it was all too much for her, did she? Was it pills or wrists?'

Zandra looks at her horrified, 'Absolutely not. It was a car accident.'

Caroline simulating zipping her mouth with bright red fake nails drawing across matching red lips, obviously recently fixed with Botox, says, 'Whoops, me and my big mouth. A car accident, eh? Hope it's not too serious,' says Caroline, unable to resist a deeply sarcastic tone.

Zandra is rattled, and it shows. She snaps, 'It was and still is, actually. She's going to be in ICU for some time I'm told.'

Caroline suddenly realises her demeanour is not helping her reason for the return to Zandra's house, and that maybe she needs to adopt a more conciliatory attitude. 'In that case, Zandra, I'm sorry. I hadn't realised it was so serious. Well of course we must both go and cheer her up. The poor, poor girl.' She pauses. 'Do you think we should smuggle in some Bolly in a lemonade bottle with some glasses, after all it's such a drag visiting hospitals, isn't it?'

Zandra is seething now. 'I don't believe you Caroline, you really take the biscuit. Just for once in your life could you be a little more sympathetic. We've been coping quite well visiting her without *boredom*.'

At that moment Hannah walks in, 'Auntie Zandra—'

Zandra's scathing tone hasn't changed and so she says a little more sharply than she intended, 'Hannah, please I keep telling you, call me Zandra. You're making me feel older than I am, and I feel pretty ancient today,' she adds, looking over towards Caroline and realising Hannah is wondering who she is. 'Caroline, Hannah. Hannah, Caroline,' she says, introducing them. Then says, 'Hannah, if you remember, is Abigail's teenage daughter. She's staying here with me while her poor mother is in hospital recovering.'

There is a fleeting recognition on the girl's face as both women look each other up and down, until Hannah says, 'Oh yeah Caroline. Seem to remember Mum mentioning you.'

A false tinkling laugh is followed by, 'All good I hope,' but seeing Hannah's stony face, she mumbles, 'and then again maybe not.' She walks over to Hannah and puts her hand through the girl's arm and says, 'Well, *we* can be friends, can't we?'

Hannah carefully disengages herself and ignores Caroline completely. 'What time are we leaving for the hospital, Auntie—sorry Zandra?'

Caroline interjects before Zandra has a second to answer and says, 'I'd love to join you. May I?' But seeing the exchange of looks in front of her, she quickly adds, 'Probably best not to crowd her out with too many visitors.'

'Yeah, maybe not,' says Hannah, coldly.

CHAPTER THIRTEEN

A week later and Abigail has been discharged. As she walks through the front door of her home, images of that whole dreadful evening flash before her; the awkwardness of the group; the angry exchange with Caroline outside; the knowledge that Baz has been cheating on her for years with Caroline; and then the awful crash.

She has been released from hospital only on the proviso that should there be the smallest anxiety or pain she will come whizzing back. 'Remember it's early days so don't start digging the garden or painting the house. You need rest and you also need to keep away from infections or anything toxic at all times.'

'Does that include enemies that were once friends?' she asks.

The doctor is young and not English, his expression is puzzled.

'It's OK, my attempt at humour. Ignore me.'

After a jostling taxi ride, they are back at home. Hannah immediately orders her mother to sit in the living room. She plumps up cushions on the sofa, insists she sits down, positions a footstool in front of her and then lifts her mother's feet onto it. 'Is that comfy, Mum?'

'Yes, but I'm not an invalid Hannah, honestly—'

'Don't argue, just for once. I'm in charge now,' she jokes.

Abigail looks around. It's almost like she's come back from a holiday and now she can relax. Except of course it was nothing like any holiday she'd ever had. The house smells musty and everything looks so shabby, she thinks. Paintwork needs touching up. And those curtains need to go. She decides she has never liked them. Particularly now, they were Basil's choice. They most definitely have to go. Get ripped to shreds first even.

Hannah pops her head around the door. 'Cuppa?'

Abigail on auto pilot starts to rise.

'No, no,' her daughter signals for her to sit back down again. 'Relax, relax. I'm making it. Stay there and behave. Here,' and she grabs the remote, and hands it to her, 'Stick the TV on.'

Abigail sighs and does as she's told, flicking through the programmes. As usual there is nothing much on, repeats, day-time TV, the news. The next minute, Hannah is back around the door again, 'Bacon sarnie all right or something else?'

Abigail wonders to herself how long nurse Hannah will be able to keep this up. By the afternoon the novelty has worn off. 'Jasmine has asked me to come over,' she says, 'I wouldn't mention it but I haven't seen her for ages because—'

'I know, because of me. Off you go, I'll be OK.'

'You sure Mum?' She hesitates, but selfishness is on the verge of winning one hundred per cent. She reluctantly suggests, 'I can stay. Perhaps I should. After all, you're only just out of hospital and—'

Abigail waves her hand, 'Go, go, go and enjoy yourself, you deserve it. I'm fine.' She looks at Hannah, puzzled. 'Hey you, stop a minute. I don't remember that top or those jeans. Are they new?'

Hannah reddens, 'Er yeah. They didn't cost much. They were in the sale. And there was a discount.'

Abigail is annoyed. She hates the thought that Hannah has been playing on Zandra's generosity. She knows exactly what her daughter is like. The sad face. The *if only* comment, when she's spotted an alleged bargain on the internet, or in a shopping mall, and then the exuberance when she's achieved her goal.

'Hannah love, what did I say about letting Zandra spoil you? How much were they? We can't keep taking advantage of her, especially when you've been staying with her all week.'

Her daughter hesitates and blusters, 'But it wasn't Zandra, it was—look does it matter?'

Abigail sits up, 'Yes of course it matters, we're not a charity case just because your father has deserted me.' She closes her eyes kicking herself. She's been trying so hard not to disparage him in any way. 'Forget I said that, I should know better. But where did you get them from?' She tries to make light of it. 'Come on, who dished out the dosh? Was it Grannie, did she send you some money?'

The girl shoves her hands into her trouser pockets and scowls at her mother. 'Before you start, you always said *speak as you find,* so don't have a go at me.'

She pauses and then admits, while looking down at her feet, 'Caroline bought them for me.'

'Sorry, I wasn't sure I heard that.'

'I said, it was Caroline.'

Abigail almost screams the name, 'Caroline! Caroline bought them for you?'

Hannah's face takes on a pleading look. 'Right, now I know you've got some weird hang-up or grudge against her from the past, but she's trying really hard to make up for whatever she did wrong when you were kids. She's been really nice to me and she says lovely things about you. She told me once when you were—'

Abigail puts her hands over her ears and yells, 'Stop, stop, stop!' She stares at Hannah and spits out, 'Weird hang-up? Grudge?' Abigail can feel her whole body tighten in stress. 'This is unbelievable.' Pain is attacking her as simultaneously she tries to moderate her tone, but still she shrieks, 'Do you know what that nasty piece of work did? She and—'

Abigail stops mid-flow. She knows instinctively that she's fighting a losing battle. Caroline has won her daughter over. What she wants to say about Caroline's perpetual infidelity is not going to help either of them. She's constantly fighting the overwhelming compunction to tell Hannah exactly what her father is like and has done but she's determined she won't act like other bitter deserted women. She stops herself wondering if that is what she is. She has been deserted. She's hopes she's not bitter as well. Is her divorce the reason why she despises Caroline so much?

'Mum,' she pleads, 'give her a chance. She's really nice when you get to know her. Zandra says she's really trying. You should let her come over here. I could cook for you both. She loves my pasta, says it's the best she's ever tasted.'

Abigail groans inwardly and thinks *How cosy, all this is. How this hurts a lot.*

'About Jasmine—'

'Jasmine? Oh, that, going out? Yes OK. Go and enjoy yourself.'

'And you really don't mind?'

She's not concentrating on Hannah. She's too wound up with Caroline inveigling herself and controlling yet another member of her family, so distractedly she says, 'No, be careful but don't be late.'

At the expense of an evening with her friend, Hannah wonders if it is such a good idea to leave her mother on her own while she's obviously in a bad mood about Caroline. Should she admit that she's been really troubled at the thought that her mother was driving in the wrong direction when the accident happened? She worries it might have been deliberate. 'Mum, you won't do anything silly will you?' she asks her.

'What?'

'No, I won't do anything silly,' she says, disappointed that anyone might think that, especially Hannah. 'I'll sit here and behave myself, watch TV, doze. Go on. Have a nice time and by the way, thanks for cleaning the house, it looks spotless.'

'Oh, that wasn't me, that was the lady that works for Zandra. I was going to do it but then Caroline had tickets for the O2.'

And there she is again. Just like a terminal disease that never leaves you. 'Of course she did.'

'Right, I'm off then,' she says and then turns back to her mother. She stands there briefly clearly wanting to say more.

'What is it? Have I got dandruff or something?'

'Mum, can I ask you something, and you promise you won't get mad at me?'

Here it comes, Abigail thinks, *she's going to ask chapter and verse about her father's affairs.*

'You know you were going the wrong way? Was that deliberate?'

Oh, she does think I did it deliberately, thinks Abigail. She needs to put her right about that right now. 'I took a wrong turning in a violent storm. I could barely see a metre in front of me. I was deliberately trying to get home without crashing. So no more talk of that nonsense please.'

'The thing is Mum, Zandra said you'd gone off as angry as hell, but then Caroline insisted she'd calmed you down and apologised to you for something she thought you might be a bit upset about in the past. I asked her what that was but she wouldn't tell me. See I know it's not that easy for you to calm down that quickly when you're angry. When Dad and you used to have rows, they kind of went on for a couple of days before you both got it sorted. So, I was wondering—'

Abigail is getting annoyed, 'Wondering what? Spit it out.'

'Were you going to do something to yourself?' She lowers her voice so Abigail can barely hear her. 'You know,' she says, tentatively, 'kill yourself?'

And there it was. Out there. Hannah's fear that her mother was going to commit suicide over her father leaving her.

Her voice trembles with emotion with the overwhelming sadness that Hannah is thinking this.

'Hannah, it was honestly only an accident. Please don't worry about anything like that and go out and have some fun with your friends.'

'But you were really angry Zandra said, so were you—'

'I was going the wrong way because of the storm and because some dumb idiot was tailgating me. I thought I'd said all this before. Is that what everyone thinks?'

Abigail holds back, mindful not to mention Emmett Ryder, who has more than likely been sleeping with the enemy, she thinks.

'No, not really. It's only because you left when you were so angry but I didn't know it was because of the man tailgating you. He could have killed you! We should call the police and get them to look at the CCTV. He should be arrested for what he did to you.'

This is not what Abigail wants at all and instantly regrets what she's said. Emmett will not thank her if Hannah involves the police. She needs to shut this down fast.

'No, we don't need to call the police Hannah. The guy was tail-gaiting me. Then he wasn't. I guess he didn't help my equilibrium. I was mad at Caroline. I regretted leaving Zandra and driving in the storm. I wasn't thinking clearly. I wasn't concentrating. Then the fox leapt out in front of me so I suppose if we should blame anyone or anything it was the fox really but I most certainly didn't try and crash the car and we don't need to involve the police.'

Hannah looks doubtful, 'Are you sure?'
'I'm sure, now off you go before I change my mind,'

she says. 'Have fun but not too much fun. No more raves. No more police. OK?'

CHAPTER FOURTEEN

'Hello?'

'Abigail? Is that you? Have I got the right number?'

'Yes, you have but it's me, Hannah. Mum left her cell behind even though I reminded her over and over to take it. It sometimes feels like a role reversal here. Do you think she dislodged some part of her brain in that crash?'

Zandra giggles. 'Goodness you've allowed her to go out then?' she asks. 'You put a curfew in place?'

'Maybe I should have. She was being a bit weird.'

'Why, what do you mean?'

'She went out all dolled up and wouldn't tell me who she was meeting. Then five minutes after she'd gone Dad phones her mobile wanting to know where she is. And, get this, he's sounded really secretive. So, I'm thinking maybe the accident was a wake-up call for both of them. It's made me wonder if they're getting back together. What do you reckon?'

Zandra doesn't want to dampen her hope but also is reluctant to encourage something so unlikely. Since the crash Abigail has confided in her that she was disappointed that even though they were separated, Baz hadn't once phoned to see how the mother of his child was. It was the final straw as far as she was concerned.

Therefore, Zandra thinks not only is it unlikely that Abigail is meeting Hannah's father, it's even more unlikely that she's going on a date with him. So where is she going?

But Hannah has become carried away with the idea. 'I'm positive I've got it right, don't you?'

Zandra hesitates, 'I suppose it's possible.'

Triumphantly Hannah shrieks, 'I knew it, I knew it. You think so too. Great that means we won't have to move and I won't have to live in some horrible old flat with a dodgy lift and babies screaming and kids shouting their heads off.'

Zandra thinks it wasn't that long ago that Hannah was one of the screaming babies and that she's still a pretty noisy kid when thinking about the rave only a week ago. Plus peace and tranquillity have returned to the house. Instead of grunge or rap or garage music, whatever it's called, she can play her Chopin and Schubert.

'It's a shame because I was going to ask if she wanted to meet me for lunch in our special place. Oh well, another time, another day,' says Zandra.

'If she says anything to you about getting back with Dad,' Hannah persists, 'you will tell me won't you even if she makes you promise not to? Please Zandra, please, I need to know. It would be such a relief.'

It will never happen she thinks but says, 'You'll be the first one I call.'

***

While Hannah is dreaming of a reconciliation between her parents, Abigail is wondering why she has agreed to meet up with Emmett Ryder? Those first few phone calls from him were not only apologetic but he seemed genuinely concerned about how she was coping. The last couple of days, his tone had shown a distinct change to more of a plea for her help in finally stopping Caroline's fraudulent ways, once and for all.

'But why me Emmett? You're barking up the wrong tree well and truly if you think I can convince her to trust me. Our friendship is history. I hate every living bit of her stretched and surgically changed body, and she knows it. In fact, I think she gets off on it.'

He turns up the persuasion, 'Don't be too sure. Apart from being a greedy confidence trickster, she's an egomaniac. She won't accept that not everybody loves, worships her and falls for her lies, believe me, I've met hundreds like her.'

'Hundreds? Really?'

He backtracked slightly, 'OK, maybe a few. Oh, all right, it was my cousin Jolene.'

'Jolene? Like the song?' While Emmett was making a cringing face on one end of the phone, Abigail had launched into a tuneless rendition of the country and western song at the other.

'You quite finished?' he asked her.

She retorted sniffily, 'If you can't take a joke maybe you should be asking someone else to help you. Goodbye.'

'Abigail, wait, please.' But she'd hung up.

She'd sat there, arms folded, watching and listening as the cell rang and then went to voicemail. After the tenth call, she picked it up, 'Yes.'

'Abigail, Abby,' he said, his voice smooth as silk. 'Please, you gotta help me. Seriously honey, please.'

After half an hour of sweet-talking, she relented.

Now, Abigail finds herself meeting Emmett under the clock in Charing Cross Station as she had done years before with many a date, including, fatefully her soon-to-be-ex-husband.

Emmett spots her before she sees him. She looks stunning and he gives a low whistle thinking, *So that's what she looks like out of bed wearing smart clothes and make-up.* He smiles to himself thinking usually that particular notion is in reverse.

He taps her on her shoulder and she twists around, 'Oh hullo.'

'Hello yourself.' He hesitates, then grins, 'Should we hug and kiss like everybody else around here. I'm feeling quite left out.'

She raises her eyebrows and says quite haughtily, 'I think not, but if you try, be warned. Even though I'm not long out of hospital I still have a fearsome right hook.'

He laughs and says, 'Point taken.'

Abigail's heart weirdly skips a beat at his smile. She considers he is definitely quite good looking in a craggy sort of way. He positively exudes charisma. A voice inside her cautions, *Careful. Remember you're bouncing right now, bouncing out of a relationship that was toxic, don't bounce into one that could be even worse. Don't forget your promise to yourself, Abigail, no more men means: no more game-playing, no more waiting by a phone that never rings, no more food thrown into the bin, and particularly no more bloody heartache.*

She decides, bull by the horns, she needs to put her cards on the table. 'Before you say or do anything else, there's one thing I have to make clear. Are you listening and paying attention? To me Emmett, because of various circumstances, you should know I see men as the enemy. The only reason I'm tolerating an association with you is because of my recently acquired vindictive streak and determination for justice against Caroline.'

'That's sad. Does *the enemy* still include me?' he grins.

'It *especially* includes you. Tailgater!'

He allows himself to be gently manhandled from the station and asks, 'Hang on, where exactly are we going?'

'You, my friend, are about to buy me lunch at one of my favourite off-the-wall-expensive haunts. And I'm most likely going to order lobster.'

Emmett wonders how his boss will take that when he hands in his expenses? Abigail had better come up with the goods.

***

Abigail is studying the sweet trolley. She feels she can indulge herself having lost a fair amount of weight on the obligatory hospital diet. Ironically, she's managed to get into the designer red dress she was going to wear the night of the accident. Not only did she not have to wriggle the zip up and down, but she has breathing room as well. *Guess what Hannah, I can sit down and am eating like a pig, and no seams are popping open.* She giggles at the thought.

'What's so funny? You conning lunch out of me or the thought of getting revenge on the home-wrecker?'

'Both.'

Emmett is about to signal for more wine when Abigail stops him. 'No, seriously, if I drink anymore, I'll slide under the table.'

'That would be a tragedy particularly as you look like a million dollars.'

She feels her cheeks going even redder than they were after a bottle and a half of wine. This is the first compliment Abigail has received in almost a decade from a man. At the thought, her eyes begin to mist over. She kicks herself mentally. This won't do. Falling at the first fence. *It's a throw-away line Abigail. Get a grip.* A sudden fleeting image of her and Emmett wrestling each other in the hotel next door sends her temperature soaring. She blinks, but the image is still there.

'Are you OK?'

'Fine,' she replies, quite snappily, instantly regretting the sharpness of the tone. After all, it's not his imagination that's running away. Or is it? She glances at him. *No, he looks just the same. Adorable. No, no, no. Not Adorable. Control yourself Abigail! Trouble is it's been a long time since she was in the arms of any man, wrestling or otherwise.*

She hurriedly puts the linen napkin to her face to hide the smile that is involuntarily and slowly spreading over her face, she can't stop herself from imagining his lips on hers.

'Coffee?'

'Let's,' she mumbles from behind the napkin. Finally, back in control, she asks quietly, 'You haven't explained exactly how all this is going to work, supposing it is going to work.' She pauses. 'If this goes the way you want it to, won't you be accused of entrapment? That's the word isn't it, entrapment?'

He looks irritated, 'Yes that's the word. Keep your voice down, people are looking, and definitely listening.'

They stare at each other briefly, both showing mutual annoyance. Reluctantly it is Emmett who feels he has to break the silence. 'I've done this before Abigail. I'm no novice here. I know exactly what I'm doing. It'll be fine if you do exactly as I say and don't go off piste.'

Abigail is even more peeved now and with her voice a whole decibel higher, she spits, 'Off piste? What's that supposed to mean when it's at home? I don't know how you can have the gall to judge me when you don't know me whatsoever. Your bizarre assessment of my capabilities is beyond comprehension. Are all you Americans this rude? I'm only here at your persistence, because you say you need me and not the other way around. But that offer of assistance, *buddy-boy, old pal,* is now summarily withdrawn.'

She makes to stand up, but he grabs her arm and pulls her back down into the chair, his expression showing more than a degree of anger. Biting her lips hard together, she lifts his hand from her arm and drops it down as if it is the vilest thing on the planet. Then leaning forward, her eyes wild, she hisses, 'Never, ever, do that to me again. I don't work for you, and buying me an expensive lunch doesn't mean you own me in any way, shape or form. Considering I was the one with the bang on the head, your memory isn't serving you too well. I thought I just mentioned that you need me more than I need you. Actually, I *don't* need you at all, or any other man for that matter. So, if you'll excuse me, I'm off. Thanks for the lunch, but no thanks for anything else.'

He looks flustered, and instantly begins to grovel, pleading with her to sit down and listen, apologising, adding that, 'You've got to understand Abigail, the thing is, I've been under a lot of stress lately.'

Abigail's eyes are even wider, she can hardly contain her sarcasm, 'And I haven't? No, course not. Let's compare lists, shall we? Has your marriage recently taken a nosedive after decades? No? Right. Did your former best friend just days ago reveal that she's been having a continual affair with your spouse even before your wedding day? No, I thought not. Did you experience a tail-gating moron in a thunderstorm who almost forced you off the road, and thereafter did you crash your car into a ditch? No. Please *don't* raise your hand as if you are about to stop me, because I haven't finished. Oh, what else was it? Oh yes, did you just have your spleen removed so that now you are subject to contracting all kinds of infection known or unknown to man? No, not that either? Well, there's a thing. Interesting. And on top of all that are you presently being bullied into possibly breaking the law of the land in order to satisfy a stranger aka tail-gating moron's dream of nailing a perpetrator? How am I doing? Up for the challenge, are we? Go on then, don't let me hold you up. Let's hear your tale of woes, shall we? I'm all ears.' Abigail puts her hands behind her ears as if to emphasise the suggestion.

Emmett looks crestfallen. He hangs his head down, shaking it from side to side. 'You got me. You beat me lock, stock and barrel, one hundred per cent.'

Abigail folds her arms, her facial expression now one of smugness. 'Fine,' she says, 'as long as we are clear.' She drains her wineglass. 'Actually, maybe I will have another little snort, I think I deserve it, don't you?'

Emmett signals to the waiter for more wine and then the bill. Then his face creases into the biggest smile possible. 'You know that list you just spouted out?'

'Sorry?'

'The list of agony you were telling me about, the ex-husband, the affairs, the rejection—'

She snarls at him, 'Are you deliberately trying to piss me off?'

He waves his hands at her, 'No, calm down. I was just simply mentioning that you missed out one important detail, that's all.'

'Really? Go on then. Can't wait for this one. Will it be a—what do you Americans call it—a doozy?'

He ignores her and instead asks, 'Tell me, when you got taken into the ICU, how do you think they matched your blood type? Guesswork?'

Her face crinkles up, and Emmett is irritated to notice how delightful her nose looks when she does her *puzzled* expression. He's trying not to like her.

'What are you getting at?' And then her expression one of horror, she whispers, 'Oh God, did they check my blood for alcohol? Oh shit, oh shit, oh shit, I'm totally fucked. Oh God and the Insurance—that means they won't pay. Oh no, they'll prosecute me. What am I going to do?' She pulls out her phone. 'I need a lawyer and fast.' She starts to search the internet.

Smugly, he answers, 'Hold on before you do that. The answer to your question did they check your blood for alcohol is yes and no. That is right. Got it in one babe. However—'

'However, what?' she asks desperately hoping he'll offer a solution.

He pats his jacket down. 'However, the blood report is no longer with the police.'

She does the puzzled look again and he has the warm glow again too, as she questions excitedly, 'So *you* have it? Really? You?'

'Yup, sure do.'

Almost under her breath she dares to ask, 'I'm not going to ask how, but have you got it safe and sound?' adding, her voice low and almost inaudible, 'And only one copy?'

'Sure thing. Safe and sound, as long as—'

Her mouth twists to one side, 'Oh I get it. Right, so it's not just entrapment you do, but also blackmail.'

'Dirty word blackmail. How about friendly persuasion?'

There is a silence between them, until Abigail asks, 'OK, Emmett Ryder, shoot. What exactly do you want me to do?'

Emmett proceeds to detail his plan, but as he does so, he thinks to himself what a magnificent creature Abigail is. He's pushed aside his reluctance at getting involved and now he's determined to find out all about her. Whereas while Abigail listens entranced by his accent, her mind wanders slightly, fantasising about what it would be like to be Emmett's girlfriend, by a pool in San Francisco. Or chasing villains with him in Central Park or maybe even in the Rockies, on horseback.

'What do you think?'

'Sorry?'

'Do you reckon it will work?' he's asking, unsure as to whether she's been paying attention.

'Yup, I'm sure you've got it all sewn up. Jolly well done. First class,' she waffles, wondering what the hell he's been saying and what she's agreed to do.

His eyes narrow at her toying with him. 'That's all you can say is it, jolly well done? What's that supposed to mean?'

She waves her hand dismissively, 'Oh I don't know.' She shrugs. 'Listen, you've got to remember, I've only just come out of hospital, I'm taking drugs and by rights I shouldn't even been drinking.'

His eyes close and he runs his hand through his hair and mutters, 'Jesus.'

But if Abigail was finding it difficult to concentrate before, her attention is even more divided now as she notices in the far corner of the restaurant someone who looks remarkably like Zandra watching her. She dismisses the notion as being totally dumb and considers it's simply the weird affect alcohol has on the brain.

***

Zandra was miffed that Abigail had made other plans. She'd hoped to surprise her friend by taking her out to her favourite top-notch restaurant, something that only ever happened on special occasions. She'd already organised with M. Bouvier to make sure lobster was on the menu, and for that reason she'd decided she had to dine there anyway, feeling it was rude and an imposition not to.

As she sits there alone, pondering whether her stomach can actually stretch to accommodate crepe suzettes, she notices a man lunching with a female, sitting across the other side of the room who looks vaguely familiar, but as much as she can wrack her brains after an aperitif, a glass of Sauvignon Blanc, two glasses of Chateauneuf du Pape, she cannot place from where she's seen him before. As she stares and watches the couple, she catches her breath when she sees the man grab the female's arm, and then it rather looks like something is about to go terribly wrong.

Concerned suddenly, Zandra looks around and realises everyone else seems too self-involved, especially with their food. No-one appears to be taking any notice of a possible impending disaster. She is about to call the waiter over, when the woman turns her head and Zandra realises with a shock that it's Abigail. This revelation confuses her totally.

'Goodness, Hannah was right. Abigail is dating. But Hannah has totally got it wrong with whom. *That* is not Baz.'

And then it hits Zandra hard, like a slap on the back of the neck.

Abigail is having lunch with what looks remarkably like the images on Caroline's phone; the photograph in the envelope; in fact, Caroline's boyfriend.
Is it some kind of revenge, she wonders? And how is that possible? She mutters to herself, 'I hope you know what you're doing Abby. You're playing with fire.'

CHAPTER FIFTEEN

It's 4 am and Caroline is busy on the computer and has been for hours. So far, she's created ten new companies on Companies House website. She's using Zandra's house as the registered address. That will change as soon as she's managed to find a dodgy solicitor willing to help. She has feelers out already. She yawns and stretches. Time for bed.

She pummels the pillow into shape. Caroline misses her emperor-sized bed with its thick memory foam mattress in New York. She also misses her apartment. And she's sick and tired of having to move around the planet when things get too hot for her.

She accepts begrudgingly that Zandra has made her very welcome, more welcome than she imagined would be possible after the way she once treated Zandra's parents. She despises her for her *niceness*. It's so boring being nice. Caroline would have had far more respect for her if, when she'd knocked on her door that night, she had slammed it shut in her face. What a fool Zandra was but she can use that to her advantage. Caroline is ruthless. She is incapable of feeling.

After ten minutes of pulling at the duvet and more pummelling of the pillow she is finally drifting off into sleep when her mobile flashes, its vibrations moving the phone close to the edge of the tiny bedside table. She reaches out and grabs it before it falls. As she does so, the ringing stops. There is a message.

'*You awake?*' It's a female caller.

Thanks to you I am.

She dials the number. 'You'd better have a very good reason for ringing me this late,' she says.

'Yeah, sorry. I had a feeling this wasn't the best time to phone.'

'And your feeling was correct. What do you want?'

The female draws in her breath. 'Nice attitude. I was calling to warn you.'

Caroline snaps, 'Warn me about what? Get on with it so I can go back to sleep, if I can. I'm wide awake now.'

'Sorry. Well honey, it's bad, bad news. You sitting down?'

'I'm in bed moron. I'm *lying* down.'

'Just as well.' The woman pauses. 'So you and Emmett are an item, yeah?'

'Oh. You're going to tell me he's cheated on me. So what? I've cheated on him. It's the way it goes. Besides, doubt I'll see him again.'

'Not so sure about that.'

'What do you mean?'

'Maybe he has cheated, maybe he hasn't. That's not it.'

'So, what is *it?*'

'You won't be so laid back when you hear who Emmett really is and who he works for. He's not the hot guy with a sports car you thought he was.'

'Really, so what is he? A confidence trickster. Now that would be some kind of irony, wouldn't it?'

'He is in a way.' She pauses for effect. 'He's a Fed.'

Caroline sits bolt upright, gasps for breath. 'Say that again! You are kidding right?'

'Wish I was honey, wish I was. Before you ask, I have this verified one hundred and ten per cent. What's worse is, he is totally onto you and what you've been doing. You need to watch your back.'

'How the hell—?'

'If you want to know who to blame, then talk to Paulie, that son-of-a-bitch Paulie.'

'Paulie, but he's a *made*-man, why would Paulie—?'

'They flipped him. Got to him though his wife and kids and his mistress. He was stitched up tighter than a kipper. God knows where they've got him stashed away but believe me, he's been singing his little heart out. The feelers are out everywhere to find him before he makes it any worse. If that guy gets to carve his Thanksgiving turkey for his family, I'll eat my hat.'

Caroline is shaking, trying to remember what she has said to Emmett that would incriminate her. Then she asks, 'But Emmett, he's still in the States, isn't he?'

'Wrong again. You sitting down?'

Caroline snaps, 'What's wrong with you? I told you already, I'm in fucking bed.'

The female, Melody, a vivacious red-headed twenty-something at the other end of the phone, toys with the idea of terminating the call right now to let Caroline sweat it out. She was Caroline's assistant until about six months ago; Caroline owes her money. It's the only reason she's touched base. She loathes Caroline but she needs the money before she's kicked out of her apartment. She figures that if she keeps her informed and things go well in the UK, money might drift back to her in California. It's a vain hope, especially as she knows the money will be dirty. But beggars can't be choosers and it wouldn't be the first time Melody had crossed the line. Juvie, was not only an experience, it was a learning curve. And so, she imparts just enough knowledge for Caroline to keep her dangling on for information she will need.

'Word is he's close, not sure where but he's hot on your trail.' Melody tries to disguise the delight she's feeling somewhat unsuccessfully.

'Shit!' Caroline says. 'You don't have to sound so joyous about it.'

Melody rounds on her, 'I wasn't. It's not doing me any favours if you get busted. You still owe me money. Listen Caroline, I didn't *have* to warn you and maybe next time I won't.'

'OK, OK, there's no need to get antsy about it. You'll get your money, you'll get your money if you keep me posted. Where is he now exactly?'

Melody taps the phone and hisses at the other end.

'Hello, hello Melody? Will you damn well stop pissing about? Tell me exactly where he is,' Caroline orders.

It's too late. Melody has clicked off. It wasn't an accident.

CHAPTER SIXTEEN

Zandra is reluctantly flipping through a property developer's brochure. It shows various ongoing developments and future projects. There are two bedroomed, three bedroomed, five bedroomed houses, semi's and detached, bungalows, flats, pent houses, in cities and in the countryside. The brochure is thick, colourful and very glossy. It could compete favourably with any up-market builder in the world. It looks professional, impressive, totally legitimate.

It isn't.

She hands it back to Caroline. 'Yes, very nice,' she says almost dismissively. 'I'm not sure it's for me though, Caroline. I realise I'm not getting a very good return on my savings, well, almost zero if I'm honest, but it's all safe. Safe and secure. I don't want to risk anything in case I can't find another husband to look after me, and all this.' She waves her hands around the room. Afterwards she stares down at herself and then pushes up the slight sag under her chin and pulls her lips tightly together. 'Men want twenty-year-olds with firm bodies now so I don't pass the test. So, no, sorry, I can't take any risks.'

Caroline smirks. 'How many husbands it is so far? Three?'

Zandra's eyes narrow slightly. She's undecided if Caroline is having a dig at her or not. 'For your information my first husband was as poor as a church mouse, and I didn't marry Sebastian for his money, if that's what you were inferring. He inherited his father's estate two years after we married.' She shakes her head. 'I miss him terribly and think of him every day.'

Realising her instinct to ridicule wasn't such a smart move, Caroline immediately, awkwardly, adopts a more sympathetic tone. 'Remind me, Zandra darling, where did it happen?' Caroline knows fine well where the hang-gliding accident occurred. It even hit the US media it was so high profile an incident.

'In the Rockies.' She sighs and looks up. 'It was such a beautiful day. The sky was almost purple it was so blue and bright against the snowy peaks. The day before he'd been white-water rafting. I wouldn't go even though he begged me to; I was too scared. Thinking about it, he did something dangerous every day of that holiday. It was bound to happen in the end.' Her eyes mist over. 'There are times, quiet moments when I'm alone, that I wonder if he was *trying* to finish himself off because he couldn't stand being married to me.'

'Oh hardly, you can't think like that.' Caroline fights against her aversion of physically touching another human being, unless it's for sexual favours, and reluctantly puts her arm around Zandra's shoulder. 'Come on shape up. You know that's a mad idea. It was obvious he loved you. Strikes me he had everything to live for. Look he was just some crazy nut who wanted to experience things before he died. What's wrong with that?' She answers herself, 'Well obviously dying is what's wrong with that but anyway.'

Zandra sniffs and gently releases herself from Caroline's hug. She pulls out a tissue from a fancy silver tissue box on the reflective highly polished Queen Anne table and blows her nose very hard. Her nose afterwards is slightly blotchy and her eyes still moist. She takes a deep breath. 'I suppose you're right. It did annoy him that I wouldn't join in ever. I'm just an old scaredy-cat, a stick-in-the-mud.'

'Not a bit of it,' says Caroline, desperate to drag her back on course. 'Right, and what do I think you should do then? I think you should be a dare-devil and give this a go. Take a risk. Live a little. I tell you these people are gold. The investment company that backs them is yielding dividends vastly above anyone else on the market.' Going for the hard-sell approach she entices, 'It's a once in a life-time opportunity, believe me. There are people queuing up to invest money with them and it's only because I'm friends with the CEO that I've got a look in and can offer it to my friends. I tell you it was an uphill battle trying to convince him to hold back, just for me.' She shrugs her shoulders. 'Look, I'm no salesperson. It makes no difference to me what you do. It's your choice but I would simply hate for you to miss out on so much money, seeing as your worried about finding a new Mr Right.'

Zandra thinks about her online shopping experiences and how many times she has ignored those *only one left* and *thirty thousand people are looking at this right now* and *ten people have bought this item in the last minute* call to actions and missed out on what she wanted. She still has reservations but it makes her think she does hate being harried or pushed. 'If I'm truthful Caroline, I'm very worried about virtually gambling the remaining capital of my inheritance from Mummy and Papa.'

Caroline blanches slightly at the mention of Zandra's parents. She doesn't want convoluted discussion. It won't help things now. 'Look, Zandra,' she says, 'I know it's been years and maybe this isn't the time to bring the matter up, but about that thing with me and your father, can I say, once and for all, that I—'

Zandra holds both hands up, 'Stop right there, please Caroline. I don't want to hear another word on the subject. It's well and truly closed as far as I'm concerned. It's the past. Goodness, what's the point of dragging it up when both of them aren't here anymore? Not to say I don't think of Mummy and Papa constantly. My father—well Papa was a bit of a scoundrel and maybe we should conclude that you have nothing to reproach yourself for. You were terribly young and truth be told I suppose I should be begging your forgiveness for his dreadful conduct. What you went through afterwards because of him, and the—,' she lowers her voice, 'and the *thing* your parents made you do, well, I can never forget it.' She adds, 'I'm not sure I should be telling you this now, but Mummy wanted you to keep it, in spite of the scandal it would have caused Did you know that?'

Caroline forces tears to come into her eyes. She's become so expert at her emotional blackmailing it's almost like pushing a button. She manages to tremble her lips slightly, her hands shaking for effect, and then says, almost inaudibly as if it's a total shock, 'No, I didn't know that. How upsetting. How different things might have been.' She stifles an imaginary sob. 'She was a good woman your mother. A very kind Christian person.'

Caroline breaks down completely now. To anyone else it would seem over top but for Zandra it's upsetting and she reaches to comfort her. 'Oh God Zandra, if I'd known that at least I had *someone* especially your mother on my side I would have gone through with it.' She looks up, her eyes wide. 'Just think, I might have been a grandmother by now, like Gwen, instead of all those years of trying and trying with my first husband.' Tears are streaming down Caroline's face. 'It was why he left me you know. He was the love of my life, but he was desperate for children. And I—well, I just couldn't manage to do it for him somehow. He married again of course,' she lies. 'I believe they have seven children. And three grandchildren.'

'Seven! Goodness. And grandchildren?'

Caroline was never good at maths and wonders if she's gone just a little bit too far with the addition of grandchildren to the equation.

'Yes.'

Both women are now almost incoherent with their sobbing. Finally, Zandra pulls Caroline into a bear hug and strokes her hair. 'I am so sorry, Caroline. I really am. I'll try and make it up to you.'

Caroline pulls away as tactfully as she can smoothing her hair back down. She hates people touching her hair. She loathes other people's fingers on it. It takes so much time to style it and seconds to ruin it. 'There's no point in either of us getting upset, Zandra. It was a long time ago. I'm over it now. Please don't concern yourself. There's no need, seriously. After all there were children in my life.' She pauses, and says quite dramatically, 'Eventually.' She sniffs, 'Just a little later than I had wanted and I hadn't given birth to them. But there you are, one never knows what's around the corner, does one?'

She brightens considerably when Zandra unexpectedly weakens and relents, 'Well I suppose it wouldn't hurt to risk a bit of capital, after all nobody's offering as much as 8% on a Bond. It is tempting. Quite difficult to refuse actually. And you really can guarantee it's safe?'

Caroline has to fight back the triumphant look in her eyes as she agrees. 'Absolutely. As safe as houses,' *although not the unsafe ones illustrated.*

Even though Zandra seems to be on board Caroline is not convinced she might have second thoughts brewing, and suggests, 'How about we take a little trip out to one of the sites? I think you'll find it quite interesting. You'll be able to meet the man himself, Michael, he's the Construction Director. Such a lovely man. Bit of a rough diamond but a heart of gold. He definitely knows his business. You'll like him.'

'Oh! Visit one of the sites?' asks Zandra, hesitantly. 'Eeek! Deep trenches of mud and all that machinery noise. I'm not sure I really fancy—'

'Oh, come on. Live a little. We could make a day of it. Hey, I've got an idea. Maybe one of the others might want to come as well. What do you think?' She claps her hand to her head as if she's suddenly remembered. 'Victoria! Or should I say Vic, so difficult to keep up with people these days. I'm sure I heard her telling Saoirse that now she's out of the Army she's looking for a house as an investment, you know for rental purposes.' She taps her nose pensively. 'I wonder. I wonder. No, I'm sure I can swing it with the boss to include her as well. It'll be tricky but what the hell, she deserves it. After all, hasn't she been defending our country for the past few years, putting her life on the line for us? We owe it to her. Hell, yes, we definitely owe it to her.'

Zandra wrinkles her nose, 'Victoria wants to buy a property to rent? Are you sure about that? I don't remember her mentioning it to me.'

'Yup. Apparently, she's worried about her savings diminishing what with the economy being so unstable and threats of zero interest or even negative interest, you know when you get charged on your savings.'

Zandra looks horrified. 'Charged on your savings? Can that happen? You can *lose* money for having money? How can that be right?'

Caroline pulls a sorrowful face. 'Yes. It is a fact, I'm afraid. I believe they did it in Japan for a while. It lasted quite a long time if I recall correctly. Of course, there was all that trouble with the Lloyds List in the 90's as well.'

Zandra nods knowingly. 'Goodness, I remember Papa talking about that. Very upsetting. Some of his friends in the Lodge were desperate. Jim Fortescue had to sell his yacht and the boys couldn't go to Eton even though their names had been put down at birth.'

'Goodness,' says Caroline. 'Whatever is the world coming to? Having to sell your yacht? And not going to Eton, how awful for them.'

Her sarcasm is lost on Zandra who continues, 'Do you know I think in that case we should get Abigail involved. She rang me only yesterday telling me that she's had an offer on the house and she's going to rent for a while until she decides what to do. She absolutely needs a decent guaranteed investment of some sort for Hannah's university fund.'

Caroline is torn. She's determined to get as many marks as she can for her scam. But Abigail? Is that a good idea? Getting her involved with her resolute negativity towards her might scupper the whole thing. If Abigail gets wind of all this, she'll most likely put the boot in with the others and then there'll be no investment from anyone. It was too much of an uphill battle with her. There isn't one iota of doubt in Caroline's mind that Abigail loathes every part of her down to her false fingernails.

Caroline pushes the notion away. It has to be a no-go. Particularly after telling Abigail that she had been sleeping with her husband throughout their entire marriage. It had given Caroline a certain amount of pleasure to feel she contributed to that crash, if indeed she had not been the main cause. Wasn't it a trifle suspicious Abigail was heading in the wrong direction when they cut her free of the vehicle? Who wouldn't get suicidal when they were told their husband had been committing adultery since their wedding day with their former best friend?

She smiles to herself inside, remembering Abigail's horrified expression as she swallowed the lie. What a loser and what an idiot to believe that Caroline had been able to maintain a relationship with Basil for that length of time. Any trusting and thinking wife would have questioned the credibility of that allegation like that. Not Abigail. She'd accepted the fiction without question. Although it wasn't an entire fiction. There were the oddly convenient sabbaticals Baz had spent with her, from time to time, when Baz and Caroline's schedules coincided rather seamlessly. Romantic interludes that Caroline had savoured above all the other interactions she'd had with various men in her life.

For Caroline, sucking Abigail into her scam would be sweet retribution for her stealing Basil from her all those years ago relegating her to the role of mistress instead of wife.

Her plan for revenge could be almost complete.

CHAPTER SEVENTEEN

Caroline casts her mind back to the week of Abigail's wedding. She had mentally ticked off each calendar day, each night tossing and turning, plotting how she could prevent the marriage from happening before crying herself to sleep with exhaustion. Basil was hers, not Abigail's. Abigail didn't deserve him. It was a living nightmare pretending to be happy for Abigail when it felt as if her heart was being ripped out of her, shredded, destroyed, pulverised. Even Fate wasn't on her side. Nothing was going wrong. The weather was forecast to be sunny. All the guests were coming. Every detail of the nuptials was going to plan. It had all been perfect. Too perfect. She had to thwart it. She had to find a way.

On Basil's stag the night before the wedding, Caroline decided to make an unexpected appearance as the stripper, her face masked. It wasn't until she was about to rip off her thong that she revealed who she was. Immediately the party turned into a free for all. The landlord's wife was not amused. She didn't approve of *such goings on,* and said so in no uncertain terms. Basil and his friends were asked to leave or the police would be called. The dismantling of the wedding day had begun.

Up until the month before their unexpected engagement, Caroline had been convinced of Basil's love for her, Caroline. Definitely *not* Abigail. Not that Basil had given Caroline any sign that this was the case. They'd been a happy three-some for a long time. Abigail was content to always have her best school friend Caroline hanging around. It was the reverse for Caroline. To her Abigail was annoyingly getting in the way of her inevitable marriage to Basil.

It confused her slightly when Abigail said one day, 'Isn't it great how we all hang out together and get on so well? Fits my plan perfectly. See Caro, Baz has loads and loads of friends and one of them is bound to be right for you. We could all get married at the same time. What a hoot,' she'd laughed. 'Always supposing he pops the question to me before I die of old age. I've hinted enough times.'

Caroline was certain she knew why he hadn't. It was obvious to her if not to Abigail. She was so stupid. How could she not realise that Basil was leading up to ditching Abigail and popping the question to her, Caroline, instead.

That awful moment when Abigail had proudly waved her engagement ring under Caroline's nose was the worst day of her life. How could she have got it so wrong? How could Baz not see he was making a huge mistake? From that instant she determined she would crush the relationship under her 4-inch stilettos. She tried everything she could think of to divide them but the two love-birds didn't budge one inch in their resolve to spend the rest of their lives together. Even the pictures she'd arranged to have taken in the pub on his stag night and had sent to Abigail anonymously on the morning of the wedding had had no effect whatsoever.

'I'm so sorry Abigail, I don't know what came over me stripping off like that. Someone must have spiked my drink,' she'd lied.

And the reaction, 'Oh seriously Caro, I'm glad it was you and not someone trying to get him into bed. It was lovely of you to give him such a good evening. It must have been hysterical. I'm quite sad I missed it.'

Caroline wondered what drastic measures she needed to take to get through to this moronic woman. There had to be another way. Something Abigail couldn't laugh off, explain away or ignore.

Then the day itself. She was running out of time. She panicked as she followed Abigail down the aisle, fighting back the tears as the organist bashed out, full pelt, Mendelsohn's Wedding march. Through watering eyes, she could see Basil standing at the altar, not even looking worse for wear, his hair overly groomed, his suit trousers slightly too long for him, draping over his highly polished shoes, his face with a soppy smile as he fiddled with the carnation in his buttonhole. She'd gritted her teeth staring at the back of the wedding dress that she reckoned should have been hers, aiming thoughts of hatred as if they were tiny daggers that would spike and stick into Abigail's bare skin. The ceremony seemed interminable. As they got to the point when the vicar uttered those fateful words, *speak now or forever hold your peace,* she had to bite her tongue hard. She wanted to yell, *because he's mine, he's mine, he doesn't love Abigail, he loves me.* She briefly imagined prostrating herself on the altar declaring her undying love. But she didn't. She descended into a dream-like state, numb, as if she'd been anaesthetised.

She picked at the Wedding Breakfast, everything tasting like cardboard. Her eyes became glazed. People kept asking if she was alright. How could she be when the love of her life was staring dreamingly into the eyes of her former best friend, now her enemy?

Then came the chance. Abigail disappeared to change into her going-away outfit.

Baz was sitting at the table, his hands around a beer glass looking mellow and fairly worse for wear. He beckoned her to sit next to him, patting the chair in invitation.

'That was some night last night. It's catching up with me a bit.' He yawned. 'Tell me, because it's all a bit of a blur, that was you in the pub wasn't it, you naughty girl?'

She'd laughed coquettishly. 'Of course, didn't Abigail show you the snaps?'

'Snaps? You took photos?' He'd looked terrified. 'Shit, wasn't Abby upset about it? Bloody hell, Caro. I wish you hadn't done that. She hasn't said anything to me but—'

She'd tapped his hand and laughed. 'Don't look so worried. She's a big girl. She took it all in good part. Told me she thought it was tremendous fun. She even laughed and said rather me the stripper than someone stranger.' She paused. 'Happy now you've got your girl?' she forced out the words through clenched teeth.

'Blissfully,' he'd smiled back. 'And when are we going to repeat this kind of celebration in honour of you, Caro darling?'

She'd quivered at the word *darling,* but now sadly understanding the word and sentiment meant nothing. He was simply being friendly.

'Soon I hope,' she'd answered. Then questioned, 'Goodness you look awfully crumpled. Aren't you changing into something else? You can't go on your honeymoon in your wedding suit. Besides you've spilt something down your tie.'

She'd grabbed a napkin and gently at first tried rubbing an imaginary stain from his tie.

'There, that's better. You do look a mess though. Aren't you going to change before Abby gets back?'

He'd pulled a face. 'I hadn't planned to. Do you think I should?'

'Oh, I think you should. Abby will most definitely expect you to make an effort. After all, she is. It's no way to start married life is it, being cavalier, or lazy.' She'd pulled him to his feet. 'Come on lover-boy I'll help you choose something.' She'd grabbed a couple of glasses and a half empty bottle of Champagne on the way to the room, giggling, 'Might as well have a last drink together before you start your life as a married man, eh?'

'Why the hell not?' he'd agreed.

He'd been like a lamb to slaughter. She'd made him sit there, meekly in his vest, underpants and socks, while she riffled through the carefully packed suitcase suggesting this and that, and urged him to,

'Drink up, you're letting the side down.' The problem was she'd spiked the bottle on the way.

By the time Abigail had come looking for her groom and finally discovered them on the bed amongst all the clothes, Baz was out of his skull. He'd pleaded with Abigail to believe him that he didn't know what he was doing. That it was all a terrible mistake. She shouldn't read anything into it. He'd begged Caroline to help him explain to his bride that nothing had happened. He kept repeating, 'I didn't know what I was doing, please believe me.' That statement was dead right. He hadn't a clue. Caroline had made certain of that. As for Caroline's part in helping along with the explanation, she couldn't find the words. She stayed silent as Baz dug himself deeper and deeper into his adulterous hole, then looked at Abigail and shrugged. 'What do you expect?' she had said. 'You knew what he was like when you agreed to marry him.'

Abigail's trust in Basil had taken a massive knock. Although she'd laughed off the naked photos of Caroline, they'd hurt her deeply, and now finding the two of them half naked on the floor, and on her wedding day, had been a little too much to swallow. It was a huge dent in their relationship.

Baz couldn't understand how easily her trust evaporated. If she loved him, really loved him, why didn't she believe him that it was just a horrible mistake? He was drunk for heaven's sake. It wasn't as if he'd been rolling around with a stranger. It was her friend Caroline! They were almost sisters! Did it actually count as cheating?

'Come on Abby, we need to move on from this. We have our whole lives to look forward to, growing old together. I love you. You love me. Don't you?'

The beginning of their life together suddenly felt more like the end. Caroline couldn't have done anything more devastating to scupper their marriage. It was a stroke of genius. It had set the boundaries. Abigail forever more questioned Baz's every move wherever he was, wherever he was going. Baz eventually had enough of it. She kept accusing him of cheating so in the end he decided that he might as well do it.

It really was as much of a surprise to Caroline as it was to Abigail that it was she he would finally wonder off with. The break-up was finally complete.

CHAPTER EIGHTEEN

The two women sit on Zandra's verandah watching the sunset.

'More wine?' Caroline asks.

'I shouldn't really, but what the hell?'

As she sips at the Chardonnay Caroline says, 'You've made me feel really welcome, Zandra.'

'My pleasure.'

'Is it? You've no idea how heart-warming it's been that all the girls have accepted my sincere and abject apologies for all my, I have to say, "alleged" transgressions against them, particularly you dear Zandra. And trusting me with your investment means a lot. It's quite overwhelming your faith in me, actually.' She sniffs, 'I never would have imagined any of this to be happening. I'd lie awake at nights puzzling over what it was I was supposed to have done wrong. Why my dearest and oldest friends were so angry with me. None of it made sense, because none of us are perfect, are we? No-one can really say they haven't made any mistakes in their lives, can they?'

Caroline looks at Zandra, her voice choked with emotion, and says, 'I don't think you understand how unique you are Zandra. You're always prepared to listen to both sides of the story, not like the others. It does hurt you know.' Her eyes mist over, she's good at that. 'Then all the business with Abigail. There are things she did to me and Baz, I can't bring myself to think about it let alone speak it. It's a lost cause. There's no way back for either of us now. Too much pain. I'm not keen to include her in this investment. I don't feel comfortable about that.'

She pours herself another glass, and downs it as if for a confidence booster. 'Of course there is part of me that wants her back into my life regardless of anything that's happened. I have nightmares about that night, when she crashed her car. I stood outside in the pouring rain, getting drenched, pleading with her not to drive in the storm. I begged her to forgive me for everything she *thought* I'd done to her. I apologised. I even exaggerated and said how every little detail had haunted me my whole life, destroyed it almost, hoping it would convince her to stay. But she wouldn't listen, Zandra.' She takes a deep breath. 'I'm not sure if I should say this.'

'Say what? Go on,' says Zandra intrigued.

'I'm finding it difficult to say the words out loud. It's about Abigail and she—no, it's no good. I can't tell you. You'll only get upset. I can't bring any more sadness to the table. She's your friend. Maybe you're her only friend. I can't take that away from her. Not now when she's obviously at her lowest point. I mean, what was she thinking that night, driving in the wrong direction? Was she—*suicidal?*' She whispers the last word as Zandra gasps in shock.

Zandra insists, 'Now you're going to have to tell me. I insist.'

'Very well.' She pauses for effect, and then blurts out, 'She threatened me.'

'What? How?' Zandra's face turns white. In all the years that Zandra has known Abigail that would be the last thing she imagined she would do to anyone, even her soon to be ex-husband.

'Yes, I can see by your expression that you're surprised. I was too. Shocked actually. Meek, sensible and law-abiding Abigail who probably hasn't even had a parking ticket in her whole life, threatened me that if I came near her again, she'd, well—let's leave it at that.'

Zandra can't believe her ears. 'But, that's crazy, especially after you spoiled Hannah dreadfully when she was staying with us. She likes you, you know. Told me she couldn't understand her mother's stubbornness in forgiving you.'

'What can I say? Stubborn and unforgiving. My very thoughts. I did wonder. I said to myself, *does Zandra know her as well as she thinks she does?* I was the closest to her for all those years. I believe I know her better than anyone, even her husband. We grew up together. We were inseparable. We were like sisters.'

Zandra is silent for a moment, thinking. She asks, 'What happened between you? Why did Abigail stop speaking to you? I know it was something to do with the wedding but she won't ever tell me what happened. She won't talk about it, she point-blank refuses to talk about it to me, or any of the girls for that matter.'

Zandra is putty in Caroline's hands. It's easy to mould the conversation. 'Are you kidding me? She told you that *she* stopped speaking to *me?* Is that what she said? Try it the other way around. Frankly, I can't tell you the story, it's far, far too upsetting.'

It's so *upsetting* that Caroline can't quite think what that story might be. Her imagination is stretching to breaking point.

'But—but—I thought it had to be something to do with Basil and you—I mean I saw the photos of you that stag night and—'

'Oh those! That was a bit of fun. She said she was perfectly happy about it at the time. Maybe she wasn't. Who knows? It was the culmination of a lot of things between us. She used to be quite different to me when we were on our own, you know. Throughout our childhood I was always quite nervous that she would flip out at a moment's notice. Between you and me, she was quite a bully. Always threatening me, especially if I told anyone what she was like.'

Zandra is horrified. 'I can't believe it, she's so, so—'

'Manipulative? Well, she is.'

'I never knew,' Zandra shakes her head in disbelief, and then asks, 'but you still haven't said what happened. Was it because of Basil?'

'You've got the bones of it. I don't want to say anymore. I absolutely can't. Let's just say I'm surprised that Basil put up with her for as long as he did. Poor, darling Basil. Things could have been so different. We all could have been so much happier.'

'I never knew. I'm so sorry.'

Caroline shrugs her shoulder. Mission accomplished. She thinks inwardly, *Let everyone hate*

Abigail now instead of her and see how she likes it. But she says instead, 'I've had worse problems, Zandra, although losing her friendship at that age was a terrible blow to me, especially as at the same time I lost the love of my life.'

Zandra screws up her nose. 'Who was that?'

Caroline hesitates for a moment, should she reveal it was Basil, perhaps that might not be such a good idea at this time, she thinks. 'Oh, someone you've never met. He's married now.' She gives a tinkling laugh, 'I think he's got fat and bald.'

'Well, that does it. I'm determined Abigail's going to make it up to you. You need investors, and I'll make sure she's one of them. Ironic really, isn't it? She treats you appallingly and yet here you are, determined to help her out. Terribly unfair, I call it. There, I suppose that's life nowadays.'

Caroline looks at Zandra and wonders how she's managed to hold on to any of her possessions when she's such a pushover. Gullible is hardly the word for it. One way or another, Caroline feels she has scored a revenge. Either Abigail is now going to be isolated from everyone at a time when she needs them most, or Abigail is going to lose all of her money. Both would be good.

CHAPTER NINETEEN

Emmett has been called back to the States and taken off the job. He calls Abigail to warn her to watch out. He's hoping, that in his absence, she won't find out that he's been sleeping with Caroline. He doesn't think she'll want to talk to him if she finds out. 'Listen,' says Emmett, 'Don't take a chance with your money.'

'Hm? What money? You think I have money? Are you nuts? I've no car. I've lost my job. I'm divorcing. I've got to sell my house, find somewhere to live and pay for lawyers. I don't have any money but the others do. Caroline's convinced them she's a sure bet. Zandra said they're really close to investing masses into her scam so what do I do to stop her? I can't let her do this, Emmett, I can't. How could I live with myself afterwards, knowing my friends will lose all their savings? You need to lock her up. You were supposed to arrest her. I can't keep quiet now. I'm going to have to say something. It all has to come to an end. Sorry but they're my mates.'

Emmett makes a decision which may cost him his pension let alone his job.

'Can you wait 24 hours? I'll catch a plane back,' he says. He has to take a risk.

'But I thought you said—'

'Never mind what I said, I'll be back as soon as I can. I'll text you the details of the flight. Can you pick me up?'

'Sure, course.' Abigail agrees without thinking. She's not supposed to drive and she hasn't got anything to drive. She doesn't know how she's going to do it, but she'll be there. Her heart misses a few beats. Emmett's coming back.

CHAPTER TWENTY

Caroline is quietly putting her plan together, imagining how it will all play out when her cell buzzes. She rushes over to it just as it goes to voicemail.

It's Melody, her former assistant, with more news.

Caroline rings back, 'Yeah, what's up?'

'Well that sure is a nice hello. *How are you Melody? Very well thank you Caroline.* How about trying that for size?'

'Those days are gone. Tell me what you know. Where is he now?'

'Are you referring to Emmett Ryder, the FED?'

'Melody are you deliberating trying to piss me off? Remember, if he catches up with me, not only will you not be getting one cent from me but I'll grass you up and you'll end up behind bars, catch my drift?'

Melody isn't worried. If she goes down, Caroline goes down and she won't want that. Caroline is a bully and a stupid one.

'Well yesterday lover-boy was back in the States,' says Melody.

Caroline breathes a sigh of relief. 'Great. Fab news. Thanks Melody, you're a star for keeping in touch.'

'Hold on, not so fast. I said *yesterday*. Today he's somewhere over the Atlantic.'

'Shit. Where's he headed? Here?' she demands with alarm.

'London,' confirms Melody. You can hear the joy in her voice.

'You sure?'

'Yes. Oh, and I have something else to tell you, if you're interested that is?'

Caroline's fists are clenching, her knuckles. 'I am. Tell me.'

'He's being picked up by a girl.'

'So he's ordered an Uber. So what?'

'No, it's definitely not Uber.'

'Who is it then, MI5? Fraud Squad? Who?' she says afraid her scam is not going to get the chance to yield a result.

'All I know is she's English and you know her.'

'English and I know her? What kind of heads-up is that? Are you mad, I know zillions of people in the UK. I was born here. I lived here for twenty years. Surely you've got more than that?'

'Nope. Gotta go.'

Caroline sits there stunned. Who is this woman? And does it matter if she knows her or not? Most likely it does, otherwise why is she picking up Emmett? But who could that be? She hasn't a clue. She closes her eyes. Then she opens them again as the room seems to be spinning around her. She's nauseous. She feels her pulse, it's racing. Is she having a heart attack? Her mouth is dry and for the first time in years she is panicking. Everything, but everything feels threatening and she doesn't like it.

CHAPTER TWENTY-ONE

Caroline is feeling stressed. She needs things to happen a whole lot faster now. She texts the group of friends. She omits Abigail. She's made the decision not to entertain negativity from Abigail. She doesn't want her to queer the pitch.

The text reads:

'Change of plan folks. I realise this is last minute and incredibly short notice but instead of Thursday's day trip to the site, the CEO has organised an evening River Cruise on the Thames tonight. It's by way of an introduction to the company. You have to come or we might all miss out.'

Gwen studies the text and ponders if she should go. It would be difficult off-loading the grandchildren that quickly but Saoirse has contacted her and she's going.

Whatever Caroline is planning, she's not going to get away with it this time.

'We need you as back-up Gwen, please. I know you haven't got a particular agenda with her like the rest of us poor schmucks but don't you want to see her get her comeuppance at long last for our sakes, if not your own?'

Gwen hesitates. Is this the time for confession? The secret hurt has been festering inside her for decades now. Not that partly she didn't bring it upon herself. Gwen was the only child of Laura and Ken Woodward and didn't she know it. All was fine when she was a small child. She was spoilt, even she knew she was spoilt, but what the hell, wasn't that due compensation, all her friends having the benefit of siblings? Particularly Victoria with all those boys. All that back-up. She had no-one, not even cousins, or aunts and uncles. It was a lonely suffocating existence. And Laura and Ken weren't that keen on sharing their precious daughter with anyone else, so it was very rare if Gwen was even allowed a friend to tea, let alone stay overnight. It had a profound effect on her. She found it difficult to form proper relationships. It was true she was one of the school girl gang of six but it was almost as if she was the part-time member. School yes, outside school hours, no.

It was hard making excuses that she couldn't join them at parties, cinema jaunts, trips to the seaside during the holidays, because she was too embarrassed to admit that it was because her parents wouldn't let her. She hated feeling left out of everything.

When it dawned on her that there was an escape hatch which she could dive through, she grabbed the unexpected opportunity with both hands. University. It meant she could leave home. Suddenly there were no barriers, light was at the end of the tunnel and approaching fast. Her parents hated the idea. They put up obstacles. 'Can't you get a job in the local bank?' they asked her. 'Mr Jones was telling me they're desperate for young intelligent girls exactly like you and inside a couple of years, you could be running the bank, or more. Colleges are not what they're cracked up to be. Drugs, drink, debt.'

But she dug her heels in. The plan had formed in her mind and nothing and no-one was going to get in her way, especially when her mother pulled the trick of, 'I didn't want to tell you this before, but your father hasn't long to live.' Right, so is that why he's always out playing golf, or attending his Lodge meetings, or enjoying an extended Sunday lunchtime pint? Really? I don't think so, she decided.

The only thing threatening her leaving was her grades. Came the mocks and she failed miserably in her science examination. It was a total shock. She'd always come top in science. She couldn't understand it.

Her mother was philosophical in her speech to her, but her delight was almost tangible. No decent grades definitely meant no university and Gwen would have to continue to live under the Woodward regime for evermore. 'Darling, have a gap year off, or even two, until you decide what it is you want to do. Your father and I are quite happy for you to potter about at home. You don't have to get a job, we have savings.'

Her heart sank to her boots. The leaded light windows were closing in on her like a prison cell.

One rainy lunchtime at school when the girls were ensconced in the gym, swapping stories about boys and giggling and showing off about what stage they were at in their relationships, Gwen collapsed in tears. She told them everything about her life and her fear that she would end up a seventy-year-old spinster alternately wheeling her parents around shopping malls or hospitals. They commiserated with her, trying to convince her to make a stand. It was no good. Her dream of an independent life was fading. Fast.

During the next month the young Gwen, her blonde hair tied back in a pony tail, her long fringe almost touching her nose allowed moments of self-pity to show on her cherubic face. She stank of defeat. One person had a plan. Caroline.

'Don't worry I'll get you through.'

Gwen remembered her amazement. 'You? Seriously? But you're hopeless at science, no offence but if I was to take a coach, I'm terribly sorry but you'd be the last on the list.'

'Who said anything about coaching? My plan is more fool-proof than coaching. Trust me.'

With nothing to lose she told herself, in desperation she'd allowed Caroline to push her into what she felt afterwards was the biggest error of judgement in her life. She trusted Caroline. Somehow Caroline had managed to get a copy of the crucial exam paper ahead of time.

In whispered tone, her eyes wild, Gwen asked her in astonishment, 'Where did you get this? *How* did you get this?' And then she'd pushed it back towards Caroline, putting her hands behind her back, vehemently shaking her head, 'No, I can't do that, I cannot be a cheat. I've got to do this fair and square. I wouldn't be able to live with myself afterwards.' Then adding, 'Besides someone will find out and then I'm finished for ever.'

For years to come Gwen would have the image Caroline's smug expression and her taunting reply. 'Fine, be a stay-at-home daughter then until you're old and grey, having had no life at all, because believe me, that's what your parents have lined up for you. It's probably why they cheered in the delivery room when they realised you were a girl. Remember the old saying *a son's a son till he takes a wife, a daughter's a daughter for the rest of her life*. I tell you Gwen if you don't take this you might as well put a gun to your head for all the life you're going to have. Kiss goodbye to boyfriends, marriage, kids. All gone. But, it's up to you. I'll leave it here. If you don't want it, shred it. I don't need any repercussions after I've put my neck on the line for you.'

She'd walked away muttering loudly about ungratefulness.

Gwen had stood staring at the paper, fighting the compulsion to tear the envelope open and learn its contents. The battle with her conscience allowed her to at least take the paper, in her mind, to protect Caroline if nothing else. That night the envelope had sat on her dressing table taunting her. She'd tossed and turned, nightmare after nightmare breaking any sleep she drifted off into. Daybreak was still an hour away when Gwen slid out of bed. She perched on her dressing table stool staring at the envelope, willing it to open itself and reveal its contents without her physically doing so.

Without giving herself time to change her mind, in a frantic rush she tore it open and let her eyes devour each question. She'd given a hollow laugh. What a cretin she'd been. Why had she succumbed to Caroline's temptation? There had been no need for any cheating. She'd known all the answers to the questions anyway. It was a strange combination, momentary relief and guilt which turned to a feeling of nausea in her stomach. Then the shame of what she'd done washed over her. Tears streamed down her face. How could she possibly take the examination *now*? Everything was tainted, her conscience was winning. But then she'd heard her mother's voice calling her. 'Gwen darling, is that you up already? Good, I think you forgot to put the bins out last night for the dustmen.'

Gwen's grades were top-notch.

Caroline was triumphant. 'You owe me,' she'd said, 'you owe me, big time.'

Gwen debated at first whether to lie and say she hadn't looked at the paper, after all she'd known all the answers, so it hadn't helped her. But Gwen was no good at bluffing, her expression always gave her away. Caroline wouldn't accept that she hadn't helped Gwen achieve her goal.

'Yeah, pull the other one Gwen, you stank in the Mocks. Admit it, I'm the only reason you passed.' There was no arguing with her, so she gave up.

The week after the gang had all left school, Gwen was at work. She'd taken a job locally before starting university and when the first time Caroline came to her for a *loan,* as she put it, Gwen regarded it as *payback.* 'Look keep it, I know things are tight with you. Consider it something of a thank-you. Although, like I keep telling you, I would have passed anyway.'

Caroline had given a wry smile, saying, 'Yeah, whatever. Keep on telling that to yourself if it makes you feel better.' At the second demand for money Gwen had explained to Caroline, 'OK, I'll loan this to you now but I must have it back before I start uni. I'm not working for fun. I need it for my accommodation. My parents aren't helping much, especially Mum.'

Caroline had shrugged her shoulders and done a veiled threat. 'Fine. But think yourself lucky that you've got a place at uni. You can kid yourself all you like but sometime soon you need to admit that it's only because of me that you're going there. I'm your saviour. And saviours have to be compensated somehow.'

'That's simply not true. I knew the answers. It didn't help what you did. It was pointless.'

'And there we have it. Ergo. The admission. You looked. You had every intention of cheating. How would you like me to tell your new university that you're a cheat and a liar? Think they'll still allow you to stay? I think not. And your parents, how will that go down, especially if I make it known, by accident. Don't think your father's Lodge members will like that too much. Might even kick him out. Goodness, it might even make the local paper, or even the local TV news. Scandal! Wow! Imagine the headline, *local businessman's daughter found cheating.*

Fear had coursed through her veins, but she'd bluffed, 'Go ahead, tell them, you can't prove anything.'

'Can't I? That's where you're wrong, missy.'

'What do you mean?'

'I filmed the whole thing. You with your little cherubic face looking all panicky but accepting the paper.'

'But—but—'

'Not so cocky now, are we?'

Gwen had countered, 'Yeah, but it's not going to do you any favours, it'll show that you stole the paper, you'd be in trouble too.'

'Oh no. I'm not so crazy. That's where you're wrong sunshine. I don't feature in the film at all, only you arguing about whether you should take it, saying *you don't want to be a cheat*. Then you stuff the envelope in your pocket as I knew you would. What a laugh. If that's not an admission of a cheat I'll eat my old school beret! Game, set and match Gwendoline. You're stuffed like the proverbial Christmas turkey. And you did it to yourself. Bingo.'

So the blackmail began, bit by bit, any time Caroline found the need to augment her coffers.

With less money than she hoped, Gwen began university life. She'd been gutted that she couldn't join the other three at their college, but at least it was far enough away that she didn't have to go home all the time to see her parents. Those first six months were some of the happiest of her life. For the first time ever, she felt free as a bird. There was no maternal eagle eye watching her every move or a paternal interrogation to deal with at the end of each day.

A life without constraints. At last.

When Geoffrey Houseman bumped into her, literally spilling coffee down her, she didn't shout or scream at him instead she instantly accepted his invitation to dinner by way of an apology. They clicked immediately. He was a total nerd, tall, gawky, unruly hair, thick black glasses, and a fashion sense of someone living in the Dark Ages. He couldn't believe his luck that this attractive teenager was now his girlfriend. It soon became clear that both of them were novices at dating with red-faced, raised blood-pressure, clumsy attempts at love-making. Using no benchmark other than themselves, they convinced each other that they had fallen in love.

Gwen decided against telling her parents she'd got engaged and all before Spring term. It was an unusually warm April evening and she was back home for the holidays. Gwen and her parents had been sitting down to their evening meal when there was a knock at the door. It was Geoffrey making a surprise visit complete with a bunch of flowers, impulsively bought from the local garage. The look of horror on Gwen's face was a shock to him.

'Thought you'd be pleased to see me,' he said grumpily.

'Who is it, Gwen? If it's the Samaritans again—' her mother was calling out.

He'd not waited, Geoffrey had gently pushed Gwen to one side and introduced himself, 'I'm Geoffrey Houseman, your daughter's fiancé, very pleased to meet you. I've heard so much about you both.'

The visit went down like a lead balloon. He was not invited to stay. There was no room apparently in the large six-bedroom, four-bathroom house. Gwen was discouraged from having anything more to do with this *weird* person. She was quizzed about her virginity, embarrassingly so, then accused of only going to university in order to lead a debauched life. Her parents insisted she give up the notion of becoming a scientist forthwith and move back home.

In desperation Gwen announced to them, 'I'm pregnant.' It was lie but she could see no other way out. After a heated discussion between Ken and Laura, reluctantly Geoffrey was summoned to the Woodward household, sat down and pressured into marriage with their formerly unsullied daughter. He was informed the ceremony should be carried out forthwith at the local Registry Office by special licence. No child of theirs was going to bring shame on the Woodward name. What would the Women's Institute say? What would the guys at the Golf Club think? What would the vicar say? What would the neighbours say?

Geoffrey was bemused by the strange U-turn from rejected to groom but he was happy to go along with it. It was, after all, *exactly* what he'd wanted all along. Finding a wife had been his sole reason for going to university. Up until he'd met Gwen, all girls had been repelled by his awkwardness and acne and it had become an overwhelming fear and obsession that he might die a virgin. He immediately insisted Gwen should not continue her education, fearful that even though they were husband and wife she might find a more suitable man to share her life with. He was philosophical in the fact he didn't rate himself much in terms of top-quality boyfriend material.

Through sheer dogged determination and a not unnatural enthusiasm for love-making from both parties, Geoffrey had managed to make Gwen pregnant very shortly afterwards. Twin boys. The following year it was a girl, and the year after that, twins again. Gwen accepted very gracefully that her university days were over. She'd escaped her parents' hold over her and being a mother had to be as fulfilling a challenge as being a scientist, she'd hoped.

The story then should have ended like all good fairy stories, the geek and the escapee living happily ever after with their many children. Life isn't a fairy story, mostly. Geoffrey proved to be a penny-pinching tyrant and a stickler for honesty. If he was given ten pence more in his change, he made a point of giving it back even if it meant costing him more than the ten pence in question to do so. He was rigorous in his integrity to the point of being practically psychotic. He would tell Gwen, 'I suppose the reason why I fell in love with you was because you'd been such a faithful daughter to your parents; always putting them first whilst your friends went out galivanting. Don't get me wrong, I like your friends, especially Caroline, she's thoughtful and a truly genuine person. You're lucky to have her as your friend.'

Then he would add on, 'By the way, Gwen, please don't forget that I had to advance you on your housekeeping last month. It does need to be paid back in order to balance our year end books.' It wasn't a joke. He meant it. 'Now these are your ledgers. The black one is for your trial balances.' She'd looked bemused. 'To check your workings are correct and there's been no misappropriation of funds.'

'What like a packet of crisps for the twins, or extra nappies, or the fact the milkman diddled me this month?' That's what she wanted to say, but she never did. There was no point.

The constant monetary scrutiny and having five children, all under school age, was beginning to make her wonder what had been so bad about living with her parents and being spoilt rotten? That old adage about the grass being greener on the other side was beginning to hit home. Hard. She began to long for those days having run away from them as fast as she could.

During those first few years of marriage, Caroline would *drop in* unexpectedly. Immediately Geoffrey's demeanour would change dramatically, preening himself, taking off his glasses and stumbling around, as Caroline fluttered her eyelashes at him, flirting with him mercilessly. 'Yes, open another bottle of wine Gwen darling.' And, 'Of course you can stay the night, Caroline. Any time. You're always welcome, isn't she Gwen?'

What could Gwen say? The visits were always accompanied by an extortion of some kind. Money, jewellery, ornaments, anything of value. Caroline was revelling at her hold over her and the grip was getting tighter and tighter as Caroline got to know Geoffrey more and more. For Gwen this flow of money at odd times had to be accounted for in the ledgers. It stretched her inventiveness to a heightened degree.

'Tell me dearest, I see here from your accounting this month an entry which reads oddly, *payment to gardener, £50*. How can that be? Surely Mr Earnshaw wasn't due to come until next month?'

She'd flimflammed around the subject. Geoffrey having not being there much during daylight hours maybe hadn't noticed how very *tall* and *straggly* the conifers had grown and that trimming them now would save doing so the following year. If they were left to grow higher it would be even more expensive.

He'd looked suspicious but accepted her answer.

One night was particularly memorable for Gwen when Geoffrey had said, 'I don't remember seeing that ring I gave you of my mother's. I noticed you weren't wearing it so I took the liberty of searching through your jewellery box. Have you lost it? I might remind you that it's a priceless heirloom that's been handed from generation to generation in my family, for centuries.'

Somehow, she managed to convince him that it was at the jewellers. The stone needed to be reset. The following day she tracked Caroline down and pleaded with her, 'You've got to give it back, he's going to kill me if you don't.'

'For goodness' sake, as if. That man's the sweetest I've ever met. Tell him you've lost it.'

'I can't. Please Caroline, I beg you. If you don't, I'll tell him you stole it.'

'He won't believe you. But fine. Have it your way. It'll cost you two hundred. It should be more, but I'm in a generous mood.'

Between selling one of her own precious rings and faking a jewellery repair bill, she managed to pay Caroline off. At that moment in time Gwen didn't know who she hated the most, Caroline or her husband. The constant looking over her shoulder and worrying when Caroline would make another demand was wrecking her life such as it was. It highlighted just exactly how mean Geoffrey was, and not only to her. Once the meanness overflowed towards the children, she'd started becoming more and more disillusioned about her marriage.

'What more shoes? And what is wrong with hand-me-downs? We must all do our bit to recycle Gwen.'

The final straw was on her birthday. He'd handed her a birthday card. Inside was a five-pound note. 'Happy birthday. I realise you might think I'm being a bit extravagant giving you a fiver this birthday, but I saw there were massive reductions in the local charity shop and I thought you might be able to buy yourself something as a combined birthday and Christmas present. You could put the change towards something for the children or possibly the housekeeping.'

She grew more and more unhappy. She began to lose weight, and not in a good way. 'What's happened to your legs, they're like spindles?' he would criticise, and then ask, 'Are you exercising too much? I know I told you to lose those baby pounds of yours, but maybe you should rethink your routine. You look like a sack of potatoes.'

She bit her tongue. Didn't he realise she wasn't eating? Hadn't he noticed that? But that would involve in him having any interest in her which obviously he hadn't. Simultaneously, gone was Geoffrey's quirkiness in dress and outlook. He was being influenced, and not by his wife. Caroline again. During the first few months of the Houseman's wedded life, Gwen had suggested maybe a lilac shirt would be a nice change, or a colourful silk tie, or possibly jeans?

"White is fine, I'm not a TV presenter. And jeans? What Levi's? At my age? Really, neither am I a pop star, Gwen.'

By their fifth wooden wedding anniversary she'd stopped bothering about trying to upgrade him to the modern world that no longer worn baggy trousers and suspenders for their socks. At the same time Caroline's demands for money stopped.

Both things were a welcome respite. She accepted her lot as a mother and provider of cooked meals for her husband, thankful at least she didn't have to fabricate excuses any more about missing monies. All at once it dawned on her that she should continue to squirrel away the money and prepare a nest egg for the future, because she thought she might need it. To make her escape. The demands on her wifely duties in bed had finally petered out to an occasional peck on the cheek. She was sure that eventually, he wouldn't even notice if she wasn't there.

It was their twelfth wedding anniversary. Geoffrey had curiously suggested a celebratory party, something that hitherto had been totally alien to him. *People* in his house! Messing things up and touching his stuff, criticising him! Good Lord no. She'd learnt that lesson one Christmas when she'd rashly invited the neighbours in for a drink. Geoffrey had gone ballistic when he'd spotted the invitations. That night he spent until the early hours covering all the furniture in plastic. An embarrassed Gwen had the awful job of pacifying a particularly toffee-nosed female, who'd queried, 'Is this cling film? Are we considered such grubby people that you have to protect your furniture from your neighbours by cling-filming it? How insulting!'

Gwen had blushed, and checking Geoffrey was not in earshot, assured her there was no slight intended, it was mostly because of her own children. For evermore afterwards she was shunned each time she passed that woman in the street.

So their twelfth wedding anniversary had arrived and everyone was buzzing around in the living room.

Saoirse looked out of the window at the rumbling noise in the street. 'Wow Gwen, I think your anniversary present is about to land on your doorstep. Looks like Geoffrey's splashed out and bought you a new motor. There's a car transporter outside.'

Gwen thought how highly unlikely that was but on hearing and seeing the sound and sight she wondered for a moment if she had misjudged her husband's miserly ways.

The front hedge hid most of the truck from view. The next minute a burly man in high viz gear banged at the door.

'Where's Geoffrey? He should be here,' Gwen asked, suddenly quite excited. A combined feeling of guilt and tenderness at her husband's quite unexpected generosity was coursing adrenalin through her veins.

Unable to find her husband Gwen raced to the door. 'Can I help you?' she asked the man excitedly.

The man shoved a piece of paper into her hand, 'Geoffrey Houseman around?'

'Can't seem to find him right now. I'm his wife, will I do?' Goodness, Gwen thought, this is like a more expensive and up-market version of a strip-a-gram. She giggled nervously, 'Can I come out and see it?'

He barked, 'See what? The low-loader?' He looked puzzled. This wasn't usually the reaction he had. 'By all means, be my guest.' Gwen followed him outside and was sure she heard him mutter, 'Weirdo, seen and heard everything now.'

The guests had also begun to gather on the front step and driveway with the children. 'What's happening Mum?' asked her youngest, Timothy.

Gwen had put her fingers to her lips, and whispered, 'Darling, I think it's a special surprise present from your Daddy.' She'd looked around anxiously peering into the crowd, but still couldn't see her husband anywhere.

She watched with mounting elation as the driver climbed down and started to operate a noisy hand-held machine which lowered one of the ramps. 'Where's your husband's car parked, love? The BMW isn't it?' he asked her.

Gwen looked at him puzzled, and then her heart sank. There was no present for her after all. He'd obviously treated *himself* to an anniversary present. Typical. She swallowed the bile that suddenly had filled her mouth. *Why did I let myself believe that he'd do anything nice for me?* she thought. She'd begun to go back inside the house, and then something struck her as odd. The two vehicles loaded onto the truck looked fairly battered, in fact one looked more like a wreck.

Ian, her second eldest child by ten seconds, nudged his mother, 'Looks like they're going to load Dad's car onto the truck. Is there something wrong with it?'

Unease grabbed Gwen. They'd only had the car serviced the previous week. Then a piece of paper was thrust into her hand—an enforcement order. The burly man barked, 'Sign here please.'

Finally, it dawned on her. The man was a bailiff.

The next couple of days were possibly the worst of her life as she saw her home being dismantled treasure by treasure. She made no attempt to hide anything away. What was the point? It had all become tainted.

She found Geoffrey's note tucked away behind his shaving gear in the bathroom cabinet. It read, 'I'm leaving you. Sorry. Tell the children it's not their fault.'

There was no explanation. Geoffrey had vanished. He'd left behind a myriad of problems. The house had been re-mortgaged twice, each occasion he'd forged Gwen's signature. There was debt after loan after debt. Somehow, he'd convinced bank managers to rubber stamp them all. That was apart from the money lenders. Gwen rejected her friends' attempts to get the police involved. Wasn't it bad enough that they all were homeless now, to then have her children face the humiliation of a father in jail? It was all too much for her to bear.

When she'd tracked Caroline down and basically demanded to know where Geoffrey was, she had received a terse response. 'Why ask me? He's your husband. Don't you know where he is? I could see this coming a mile off, I'm astonished you didn't. You should have studied his needs more.'

The next few days were like a see-saw. She felt relieved to be free of him. She'd hadn't realised how suffocated she'd been under Geoffrey's dominant rule. It had been far worse than anything her parents had done. But she was a mother of five young children, none of them yet teenagers and she had no income.

'What are you going to do?' everyone asked her.

There was nothing for it. She had to return home. It was like a Monopoly card, *go to jail, do not pass go, do not collect £200.* Her parents were scathing at first. She was made to suffer constant recriminations and *I told you so's*. But living with Geoffrey had toughened her up.

She was positive they were ecstatic at her return even though they pretended otherwise. The most bizarre and infuriating thing for Gwen was that her parents had a completely different attitude of freedom towards her children. They encouraged the two eldest boys to *ride their bikes* and *join the local cadets*. Gwen put it down to gender at first, but when the middle child, Elizabeth turned twelve and was allowed to have sleep-overs, it rankled a bit.

She challenged her mother one rainy afternoon, and the reply was, 'It's easier when they aren't your own. After all, you're the one with all the responsibility. We can just enjoy them.'

She had no answer to that. Besides, they were her built-in baby-sitters allowing her to re-join the adult world once more. She then trained as a paralegal where she met Stephen, a high-flying barrister. Nervous of a commitment that would turn as sour as her first marriage, it was years before they moved in together. Still mindful of disparaging views from her parents that she was living in sin, it was a complete surprise to Gwen one time, a few weeks after her father's funeral when her mother announced, 'I think you're doing the right thing living together. Give it another few years before you make a final decision.'

'I thought you didn't approve of *living in sin*,' she'd replied in astonishment.

'Those days are gone.' And she'd admitted, 'I always thought your father was far too strict on you but I was too scared to go against him.'

Now all those years later, as a mother and a great grandmother, Gwen looked back on her life with many regrets but a lot of pleasure. Her life was ticking along nicely now thank you very much. She wasn't sure she wanted to stir up the past, to admit her feelings, to tell Saoirse that she thought Caroline had been the catalyst in making her and her children homeless. It was also a matter of pride.

She told Saoirse, 'I'll text you if I'm not coming.'

Gwen spent the long arduous night staring at the bedroom ceiling while her husband Steven snored and fidgeted alongside her.

CHAPTER TWENTY-TWO

It had been a long, hot summer, stifling days, difficult to breathe, oppressive nights when even lying under the thinnest sheet at night proved too heavy. It looked as though the record-breaking heat was finally coming to an end. The forecasters are predicting torrential rain and heavy floods within twenty-four hours.

Caroline prays the storm will hold off at least until morning. The boat ride is crucial to her plan; she has even hired a few actors to make it less obvious she is targeting her old school friends. Her focus is Zandra, the one with financial clout but they all have money. Caroline wants all she can get.

That hadn't been the plan originally. Emmett's seemingly relentless pursuit of her had messed things up and for the first time in a long while she is nervous. What if Zandra doesn't invest and the others follow suit? She'll be out of pocket having hired the boat, the captain, the rent-a-crowd. And what if

Emmett turns up and spoils the scam? She hopes he is as stupid as she believed he is and that he will fail in arranging an extradition order in time, if at all. He really has no solid evidence. It is he who has no hope.

Her hands are shaking as she attempts to apply her eye-liner. 'Get a hold of yourself Caroline, you've done this over and over again. It can't go wrong,' she tells herself.

Her cell pings. It's Victoria.

'Problems this end. Is 8.30 too late?' it reads.

Caroline wants to scream. She knows Victoria and Saoirse are coming together. She texts back, 'Any chance you can make it for 8pm?'

It seems a lifetime before the answer comes back, 'Yeah, hopefully. See you there.'

Zandra knocks on the door, 'OK to come in?' she asks.

'Sure.'

Zandra twirls in her outfit. She wants to know if she looks OK. She has new designer jeans, jacket and has even bought boat shoes for the occasion. She's excited. It's a good thing for Caroline.

'Stunning,' says Caroline. 'Have you lost weight this week?'

Zandra beams, smoothing down her protruding stomach, turning sideways and pulling in her buttocks as much as the bulges will allow. She looks in the mirror. 'Do you think so?' she looks across to Caroline. 'I have been cutting down on the in-between snacking.'

'Well, it shows.' Caroline thinks she looks the same as last week but hey, she's on a charm offensive. 'And your hair looks amazing too. Who is your hairdresser, I must have her number?'

Zandra plumps up the ends with her hands. 'It's a he actually, Pierre. He's a miracle worker.'

Caroline nods. She looks at the time. 'I suppose we'd better get going.'

***

Captain Peterson's week had started badly. He'd heard through the grapevine that the company was being taken over by a large conglomerate. His job is at risk. He is worried and could do without any more worry in his life.

The wife hasn't taken the news at all well. She'd set her heart on a having a large summerhouse built at the end of the garden, a place where she could *do her exercise, paint, read in peace, ask her friends around.* Now that isn't going to happen. Neither is the holiday to Las Vegas she's been hinting about. She exploded when he told her the news and she shouted that he was useless and she wishes she'd never married him. He's had enough of her nagging. He'd volunteer to join the trawler fishing fleet but he's too old for that now. He'd do almost anything to get her off his back.

When Captain Stuart Petersen is this depressed his preferred companion is alcohol. Since Monday he's been hitting the bottle hard. Now it's Friday. He's good at hiding his drinking but his second-in-command is asking too many questions, he's become suspicious.

That morning Petersen is officially sacked.

'It comes to us all eventually,' said his boss. 'They've kicked me out too. I'm on the scrap heap just like you.' But his boss's scrapheap is worth several million; it's how he attracted that young wife of his. Petersen feels bitter and he desperately needs another drink.

It doesn't help to be reminded that, 'You've got your pension, Peterson old boy, that'll help.' Trouble is, he stopped paying into it years ago. In a way it's a blessed release, he hates his job. Trudging this boat up and down the river all these years with drunken morons asking if they can steer it.

Tonight will be worse. It's his last night. The drunks will mostly be women. Plus there's a storm coming in.

The organiser, an annoying female called Caroline has somehow got hold of his direct number and has been bombarding him with calls. He's had enough of high maintenance women. He is tempted to tell her to *do one*.

However, instead he grits his teeth. The time has come for the so-called jollifications to begin. Every guest has a plus-one. The boat is over-loaded. He tries to explain to Caroline that some people will have to get off but she is ferocious, so he retreats. What does he care? It's his last night. The worst that could happen is the boat might sink. He simply can't indulge in yet another row with another argumentative woman.

No-one gets off the boat.

'Goodness, who are all these people?' Zandra asks in astonishment. 'Is it safe to have this many people on board?' She is visibly concerned.

Caroline is anxious also but is split. She needs a crowd. She also isn't prepared to back down in front of the Captain after the row they had earlier. After all, boats like this have parties every night. They go out. They come back. Nothing happens. No problem. She won't be sticking around much longer if she gets all the money. She doesn't care if the boat is currently illegal with the weight of all the passengers who all, she thinks, will have cash to hand over. 'It's a very popular Bond they're selling here,' she tells them. 'But don't worry, no-one will get left out if I've got anything to do with it. Trust me. I'll get you in.'

Saoirse, Victoria and Gwen are all now up to date and fully informed of Abigail's intention to scupper Caroline once and for all. They know all about her scam.

Zandra, who has been historically hopeless at discretion, is unaware of the reality. She is dazzled that people seem to be falling over Caroline to sign up to her investment opportunity and even more dazzled by the running videos of the property portfolio Caroline has playing over the bar.

'It's all very impressive, Caroline,' she says.

'Yes, isn't it?' Caroline lies. She feeling a lot more confident now. Things seem to be going well. 'Don't spread this around,' she tells Zandra, 'but between you, me and the gatepost, the CEO has made me a very rich woman. Just one small confession, and I didn't mention this before purely because I don't like to boast, but, well, because of him, I now own an entire block of apartments on the waterfront in Florida.'

This wasn't a total lie. Ten years ago, Caroline had been receiving more than a few rents from a Florida condo. That was until they all started to feel the heat from the Feds.

Zandra is taken in completely. She beams, 'Goodness me. Florida? Wow! I've always fancied a trip to Florida.'

'Well, be my guest. You just say the word, and I'll book the flight.'

Before long Saoirse, Gwen and Victoria have joined them. Caroline does the usual air kissing, and sucking up, complimenting everyone on their hair, make-up, clothes, etc. She peers around and says, 'Look, if you'll excuse me, I just need to find Brian, the CEO. He's simply *dying* to meet you all. I've told him *all* about you.'

Zandra watches Caroline push her way into the crowd. She grabs hold of one of the so-called competitive punters and asks, 'Where's Marmaduke?' She barks at him aggressively. 'Don't look so confused, Marmaduke Hughes?'

'Oh, you mean the Duke?' he says. 'He's probably downstairs doing a line.'

Great, thinks Caroline, *that's all I need. Actors doing drugs. Isn't the free food and booze enough for these people?*

As she pushes through into the toilet, a man is in the process of pulling up his fly. He shouts loudly, 'Watch out boys! We've got a visitor. A *lady* in the gents. What you here for darlin', some of this?' He takes hold of his crutch, shaking it up and down, receiving hoots of raucous laughter from a couple of men standing in front of the urinal.

A voice from behind snaps, 'Pack it in Sid. She's the boss. Shall we?' He's "Duke". He ushers Caroline outside, into the tiny corridor.

'What's up? You don't look happy. Thought you'd be pleased how many people I managed to round up.'

Caroline snaps, 'You do realise there's a limit to the amount of people allowed on these boats, don't you? Are you trying to sink it and drown us all? I'm not paying everyone. Hope you realise that. I said six couples max and this looks more like a bloody stag night.'

He looks shamefaced. 'Sorry Caro. Thought you say minimum. Well, I won't be able to shift them now, they're up for a party. I can't kick them off, we're moving off soon. What do you want me to do?'

'Control them. It's a shambles up there. They're supposed to be people looking to invest, not asking where the fucking DJ is? Didn't you brief them properly? They're actors aren't they. Tell them to act!'

The fifty-year-old runs his hand over his bald head, and answers nervously, 'Well yeah, some of them are actors, that's true.'

'How many?'

'Couldn't say for sure,' he hedges.

'Try.'

'Maybe three or four.'

'Three or four? You shit-head. You promised me you wouldn't let me down. This is crucial Duke, crucial.' She shakes her finger in his face. 'If you fuck this up, we're both dead. If I don't nail this, you and those morons up there don't get a penny. Is that clear enough for you?'

'Come on Caro, there's no need to lose your rag with me. And remember,' he says, doing a retaliatory finger pointing back at her, which she angrily pushes away from her face, 'I haven't paid them anything yet. If they get wind they're getting nothing, things could turn very ugly.'

She sighs. 'Whatever.'

'Yeah, whatever.'

Caroline suddenly panics and turns on the charm. 'OK, maybe I over-reacted. It's simply—oh it doesn't matter. Right, are you ready to be the CEO? Game face on?'

Duke curls his top lip as his eyes glaze over. He shakes his head. 'Seriously? Do I have to?'

'Yes. Come on, let's go get them.'

CHAPTER TWENTY-THREE

Abigail looks at the Solari board in Arrivals as it constantly updates flights. Landed. Delayed. Baggage Hall. Cancelled. She stopped biting her nails years ago but now is annoyed to find herself nibbling away at her thumbnail.

She got here early, terrified the taxi would be late picking her up. Emmett's flight was due in an hour ago. She says to herself, 'Well it can't stay up there indefinitely, can it?' Fingers crossed he'll land soon.

After six coffees, none of them decaf, she is more on edge than a sole prison guard accompanying six serial killers to the local nursing home. Her hands are shaking and her heart is pumping hard.

'Calm down,' she keeps telling herself, 'It will be all right.'

It worries her terribly that Zandra has been left out of the loop. What were they thinking? What if the others didn't manage to turn up on time and the boat steams off without them? What if Zandra entrusts all of her money to that toad Caroline? How could she get it back? Some friend she'd turn out to be if that happened and after everything Zandra has done for her and her daughter Hannah lately.

Abigail tries to convince herself that the only reason she is desperate for Emmett to land is purely so that he can shut down Caroline's operations once and for all. She can't ignore wanting him to grope her just a little bit. Then again, maybe not. She isn't thinking straight right now. It's the caffeine, she tells herself.

She wants nothing more to do with men. And not an American. She can't do short distance relationships so she'll be useless at long ones. She couldn't move over there. How would Hannah feel living thousands of miles away from her father? Not that her father would be bothered about it. No, she can't think like that. She's being unfair.

Besides, she hasn't even held hands with Emmett and already her imagination has put a new ring on her finger. Must be the coffee. Had to be the coffee. Usually is. And watching so many reunions at the arrival gate. Ugh. Slobbering. Full on groping hugs. People. Can't they wait until they get home?

She looks at her watch. They aren't going to make it. And then the Solari board clicks down again, ticking-ticking-ticking, annoyingly slowly, until it stops.

She stares at it in horror. The flight has been diverted. Her heart sinks. What should she do? Telephone everyone? Frantically she calls each of her friends no-one answers. It's either too noisy on the boat or they don't have a signal. Great.

Abigail is slumped on the super uncomfortable lounge seat, her face ashen with worry, redialling and redialling, muttering, and torn between staying in the airport or making a dash on her own to the boat, when suddenly a hand lands on her shoulder making her jump in alarm.

She looks up.

'Waiting for someone?' says the voice.

Abigail leaps up, 'Emmett. Emmett, you're here, but—'

'Yeah, of course I'm here, like I'm supposed to be right? That's why you're here too? Or am I dreaming?'

She beams at him.

He grins back. 'Now, tell me, have we known each other long enough for the hug and the friendly kiss? Or is it too soon?'

Shyly she allows him to put his arms around her, taking pleasure in the comfort of his body next to hers. She upturns her face, avoiding puckering her lips, in case it is too obvious, curious about what could happen. Her hunch is correct, Emmett, also unsure, kisses her cheek.

As they break away, Abigail stutters, 'But I don't understand—the notice board—the flight—it said, diverted?'

'Got an earlier flight. Come on, I've got an Uber organised. Let's go find it.'

***

'After you,' says Emmett, holding out his hand invitingly. Abigail does an eyeroll. As they squeeze through the noisy crowd Abigail stares at Emmett again, for the tenth time.

'Seriously Emmett, don't you think you should ditch the disguise now? You look ridiculous.'

He adjusts the wig slightly, wobbles the glasses and grins, attempting a posh English accent, 'Righty ho. What! Anything you say old gal. Super day for a boat ride, what?'

'Yeah,' she leans over to him and says in his ear, 'Can I say, you look as much like a business tycoon as my plumber. Seriously, bin the dodgy moustache. In fact, bin the lot. And drop the phoney English accent. You sound like Cary Grant doing an impression of Tony Curtis doing an impression of Cary Grant.'

'Eh?'

'Some like it Hot. Marilyn Monroe, Jack Lemmon—'

'OK don't lecture me on monochrome movies. I'm an expert.'

'Fine. Well, be an expert in dumping the disguise and the dodgy accent and be yourself.'

'Not until the boat's sailed.'

'God, that sounds a bit prophetic.'

'Maybe it is. Come on, mingle, but not too close to Caroline. It's good there's so many people on board.'

'Too many people! Very, very crowded. It doesn't look very safe to me.'

There is a sudden blast on the hooter followed by a cheer as everyone realises, they have started the cruise.

Abigail nudges Emmett. 'I've really got the colley wobbles. I don't ever remember being this nervous, my stomach's in knots. Do you think this is going to work? Please make sure none of my friends lose their money, otherwise—'

He puts his arm around her and squeezes her shoulders. 'Honey, trust me.' And this time, he bends down and kisses the top of her head, which electrifies her spine causing her knees to wobble.

She thinks to herself, *If only this was a different time*, but that word *trust* slams her back down to earth. 'Trust you?' she mutters. 'Trust a man? I'm not falling into the same trap all over again, thank you very much.'

Thankfully he doesn't hear her comment in all the hubbub.

There's another blast on the horn, followed by yet another cheer as they pass a cruise boat in the other direction. Everyone is madly waving. Emmett shouts over the noise to Abigail. 'What did you say?'

'Don't worry, it wasn't important.'

Ten minutes later Emmett has removed his disguise and is hovering behind Abigail as she makes her way towards Caroline; she's mid-stream, doing the hard sell.

Duke has weirdly adopted an American accent. 'Shucks, Caro, I think all these *fine* ladies know a bargain when they see it but—'

Emmett slaps him on the back, 'Hey, that's a great accent you got there, man. Where do you hail from? Mid-West, New York or are you a Southerner? Just fine, mighty fine.'

Duke jumps out of his skin at the suddenness of the slap. His East London tongue kicks in. ''Kin 'ell mate,' he says. 'You frightened the bleedin' daylights outta me. You wanna watch bashin' people on the back like that. Where I come from that might gain you a bunch of fives in the gob.'

'Whoops! So not so U.S. of A. after all!'

'Oh, you can—'

But before Duke can say anymore Caroline steps in with her fake laugh. 'Honestly these two boys! They're always messing about so much. Ignore them, girls. I'll have a gentle word with them.'

Before either of them can say or do anymore Caroline grabs both men by the arms and steers them at speed through the centre of the crowd, which isn't easy to do.

She snarls at Emmett. 'What the fuck are you doing here?'

'Might ask you the same question, *Caroline*. Done the deal yet?'

'What's it to you? You, sunshine, have no jurisdiction in this country. You can do one. Understand the lingo, it means—'

'I know what it means. You don't have to spell it out for me. And you're wrong honey-bun, so very wrong. Because in here,' and he taps his jacket, 'I have a warrant for your arrest.'

Abigail has caught up with the group. Caroline turns and sees her. 'What's she doing here?'

'Why shouldn't I be here?' asks Abigail with a fair degree of bite to her tone. 'You did tell Zandra you'd apologised to me for everything, didn't you? So, why shouldn't I be included in your wonderful get-rich-quick scheme?'

'Piss off.' She turns to Emmett, 'Have you slept with her yet? Bet you didn't tell her that we were an item, did you? That we'd had a *thing?* No, from your face Abigail, I can see it's come as a shock. Oh dear, have I upset the apple cart? Got in there first *again.* Tried him out in bed before *you* had a go on him? Deja bleedin' vu, Abigail, deja vu. And Emmett, you're bluffing. You're a 110% liar. If you had a warrant for my arrest you wouldn't have waited until I was onboard this boat.'

Caroline stops suddenly realising everyone on the boat has gone silent, and Zandra and the other girls are now close by, each of them not looking at all surprised. Frankly, a little smug. Caroline turns white. She spits at Zandra, 'You bitch, all of you are bitches, you've tricked me, but it's no good, it won't work, nothing's been finalised. All this had been for nothing. I'm home free. You can't touch me.'

Zandra looks confused. 'I don't understand, I thought this was—'

'Don't worry Zandra, I'll explain everything,' Gwen says, pulling at her arm.

'But—Caroline—and this American—?'

Emmett moves towards Caroline, while she shouts, 'Keep away from me, all of you, keep away from me.' She snarls at them, 'Have you any idea how much I hate you all. You, *Vic,* Victoria, with your pathetic coming-out, so what? Everyone knew you were a lesbo at school— what did you think was going on with Wiggy? You Saoirse, with your sad little teenage grudge. And Zandra with your designer shit— do you know how ridiculous you look? Mutton dressed as lamb. And as for you Gwen with your—'

Suddenly the boat shudders and there is a strange grinding noise. It starts to list. There is panic. People are pushing and shoving each other out of the way. The siren sounds. A voice comes over the tannoy, 'Abandon ship, abandon ship.'

***

Captain Petersen's young second-in-command, Alan Fraser, looks at the hunched figure slumped in the swivel chair in front of the boat controls and shakes his head. He thinks to himself, *this is going to be another long day by the looks of things.*

'OK Stu? What's up mate?' As if he needs to ask. He's heard chapter and verse about Stuart Petersen's marital problems. He even knows the dimensions of the summerhouse; it's been ground into him enough times, how it's only just within the margins of planning permission and how difficult it will be to heave it over the attached garage on the side without damaging next-door's property. The awful neighbours. And then the spiel about their noise, drug-taking, drinking, children! For Alan, it's been a rather galling experience. Stuart though, has never been interested, not once, in Alan's life. Alan's wife has been experiencing labour pains for the past week on and off. That evening she pleaded with him not to leave her, not to go to work.

'I can't do it, love. I've already called in sick twice this week. I can't do it again.'

'Well,' she'd insisted, 'tell them the truth. Can't you, tell them the baby's due today? Surely they'll understand?'

He'd sighed. 'I could, but then that's going to come off the time I'm allowed on paternity leave. Besides, love, both times have been false alarms. I've got the whole weekend off, so it's bound to happen then.'

He'd kissed her on the head and said, 'Don't worry I won't let you down. If it looks like it's the real thing this time, ring me, or text me straight away and somehow, I'll get there, even if I have to get the river police to boat me there.'

Stuart swivels around in his chair, and stares at Alan, his face drawn. 'I've been advised that I shouldn't be telling you and the crew this, but it's not like they can do anything else to me if I do. It's a fucking joke.'

Alan looks at him puzzled and then closing his eyes, he claps his hand to his forehead, instantly realising that all of those rumours are true. 'So how long have we got?'

Stuart pulls back his tatty uniform sleeve, with its threadbare cuffs, shifts his glasses to the top of his head and screws his eyes tight as he studies his watch, his mouth turned down at the corners. 'About four hours,' he says and in a defeated tone, 'give or take the tides.'

The young man stares at him in disbelief, 'You're kidding?'

'Wish I was old son. We're shrapnel as far as the new conglomerate is concerned, dust under their shoes, or more appropriately, water under the bridge. We don't matter one jot. Word of advice, seeing as your baby's due at any moment, I'd leg it, be with your wife, she needs you. Don't look so worried, I'm not going to say anything to anyone, why would I? You're a good chap, you'll do well, not like an old has-been like me.'

Alan is amazed, he'd figured that Stuart had no idea he was about to become a parent, and he's even more amazed at the suggestion he should literally *abandon ship*. For a brief moment he is tempted. He weighs up the options; his last night at work, then he leaves with a good reference; or being at Sandra's side. But chances are the baby won't come for days yet. He studies Petersen's posture and his glazed eyes, a silver flask protruding from the captain's jacket pocket, a definite sign that he's been drinking even more than usual, he realises it's a no-brainer. He has to stay to on board, there are lives at risk, the crew and not least, the passengers.

'Nah, you're all right Stu. Won't happen tonight.' He slaps his boss on the back, 'You never know, this might all be for the best. You hated this job, and once the word's out you'll be snapped up, what with all your experience at sea and on the river.'

Petersen shakes his head, then brazenly takes out his flask. He offers Alan a nip. The young man takes the flask out of politeness more than anything but he stops and says, 'Why don't we put this in the drawer for later, sort of celebratory drink to say *up yours?*'

The older man snatches it back, 'No I don't think so,' and staring at Alan defiantly, he takes a long, long gulp of alcohol, some dribbling down both sides of his mouth, which he then wipes with the back of his well-worn sleeve. 'Right, if you're too stubborn to take my advice, I suggest we get underway, the sooner we start the sooner we can finish and I can go on a bender from which I hope I never wake.'

It's half an hour after the stipulated boarding time, the engines are warmed up, ready to go, Alan is back on deck, overseeing the casting off. He hears the klaxon as they are on their way followed by a loud cheer from all the passengers, who look already to have had a skinful by the sounds of it.

Alan makes his way back up to the control room. Petersen has somehow rigged up the wheel so his hands are free, while he struggles to pour whisky from a bottle into his flask; his hands trembling so hard most of the alcohol is missing the flask completely and dribbling all over his trousers. In the end, he gives up and takes a swig from the bottle. He catches sight of Alan's horrified expression in the reflection of the wheelhouse window and swivels around, 'Oh dear, looks like I'm busted,' he laughs, but there is no warmth in it.

'Why don't I take over. You look a bit tired, Stu.'

'Piss off! I'm the captain of this shit-hole, not you.' He bangs his chest with his hand, dust flying out of the shabby uniform.

Alan makes a stand. 'I'm not leaving you in control while you're drunk. There are lives at stake, mate. Move aside, please, Stu.'

Cuddling the bottle close to his chest Stuart Petersen snarls, 'Mutiny, eh? Mutiny on the river. Bet that's never happened before. You'll make history old lad. Probably make a film out of it. Trouble is, I'm not budging.' He downs some more. Alan walks over to him, tentatively. Petersen says, 'I told you not to be here, I told you it was all over, but you chose this crate over going home to your wife. And now you want to be the hero, rescuing the passengers from the old drunk. Well, it's too late matey, it's too—'

The conversation is interrupted by Alan's cell phone. He pulls it from his pocket, his face ashen. It's his pregnant wife.

'Well, go on, answer it, don't let me get in the way. Tricky though, eh? Tough decision, baby or mutiny? Which is the most exciting?'

'Hello love, you OK?'

'I'm at the hospital Al, I think this is the real thing, can you come?' she says.

'I, er, I don't know, it's, er—'

His wife stops talking for a minute and he can hear her blowing hard as she tries to control her labour pain, and then through gritted teeth she shouts, 'I knew this would happen. You promised.'

'It's not that easy, see the thing is—'

Petersen leaps from his seat and snatches the phone from Alan. 'The thing is, my dear, your beloved husband is trying to save everyone from an impending disaster. The captain's lost his bottle, or rather should I say he's found his bottle, or maybe even two.'

Alan snatches the phone back. 'I'll get to you somehow. I've got to go. I love you Sandra, I'll always love you. Remember that.'

Sandra is screaming down the phone. 'Alan! What's happening? Alan, don't go, don't leave me! I love you too, Alan! Alan!'

Those are the last words Alan hear before the boat grinds then lists, the wheel wildly swinging backwards and forward, Petersen standing there bemused, Alan fighting to take control of the ship.

CHAPTER TWENTY-FOUR

Like all the best disaster movies, the storm breaks at the exact moment when the riverboat, no-one at the helm, crashes into an oncoming barge, the terrified bargeman having waved frantically at the riverboat, sounding his klaxon to no avail, and then fearful for his life, jumps into the water and heads for the shore.

At first not everyone realises anything is wrong, they are too busy drinking and dancing, one of the rent-a-crowd mob having turned on the riverboat's stereo.

Victoria asks, 'What the hell was that?'

Emmett shouts over the noise, 'I think we've hit something.'

The boat starts to list. This definitely gets the attention of most of the revellers onboard. People are sliding into one another with the inevitable, 'Watch where you're putting your feet, idiot,' remarks.

The klaxon starts its continuous noise as a voice over the tannoy shouts, 'Abandon ship, abandon ship.'

One couple, high on drugs, repeat the order, at the same time screaming with laughter, until someone nearby threatens to punch their lights out. Things are turning very ugly. There is an unruly scramble from some of the party-goers to get off the ship as it dawns on them that this is not a drill, it's serious, something has gone very wrong.

Seconds later the air is filled with everyone shouting or screaming for help. Emmett somehow manages, with tremendous difficulty, to stand on a table which is perilously sloping. 'Ladies and Gentlemen, please stay calm. You'll be safe if you do *exactly* what I tell you to do.'

'Safe? How? We're sinking!'

'Who the hell are you? You're not the captain. Where's the captain?'

'I can't swim!'

'Don't listen to him he's a moron.'

'Lower the lifeboats! Women and children first.'

The last instruction, most likely in jest, immediately hits home and galvanises everyone to move in that direction. Emmett concludes he's wasting his time. They aren't listening. They are all too drunk and too petrified. After one more unsuccessful attempt to control the mounting chaos, he decides to concentrate on his immediate group. He looks around. 'Where's Abby?'

However, it is not only Abigail who is missing. Caroline has vanished too. She's taken full advantage of the emerging boat disaster to escape Emmett and the hand of justice.

Emmett grabs Victoria's arm. 'You, get these women out of here. I'm going to look for Abby? Where did you last see her?'

Zandra, her face wan, closes her eyes momentarily and her voice, hoarse from screaming, mouths, 'Oh God, Oh God. She's downstairs. She went downstairs to the toilet. Please, please you've got to save her. She's my friend.'

The boat is listing very badly now, there is panic everywhere, smashed plates, broken glass, cutlery is sliding and building up around everyone's feet, making it even harder to walk. Decorative basketwork hanging from the ceiling is now at right-angles.

The noise is deafening. It's difficult to think.

Victoria has been trained for such events. She mentally puts on her Army hat and musters them together, skilfully manoeuvring them through the crowd. She steers them to the railings of the riverboat and helps them over the side. 'Get away from the boat as fast as you can or it'll pull you in as it sinks!' she shouts. They are not alone in taking notice of Victoria's suggestion. Zandra crosses herself as she leaps into the darkness, bizarrely wondering if she should do breast stroke or crawl. Flashes of lightning occasionally illuminate the disaster scene, spotlighting people swimming frantically who only moments had been drinking, singing and dancing.

Water is now gushing into the boat from the gouge in its side and the river is taking full advantage of claiming the riverboat as its own. On the sloping deck a small pile of people lie, motionless; they have been trampled on by those trying to escape. It's possible some in this heap would survive, if treatment were immediately available, but nowhere is help close at hand. Villains and involuntary heroes alike are presently thrashing around together in the darkness of the choppy waters. In shock. All now suddenly sober. Some cursing their God. Some praying to their God. But all are wondering if it is their imagination or not. Can they hear the faintest sound of sirens wafting in and out through the wailing notes of the storm? Is it their imagination? Is it their overwhelming desire for salvation kicking in?

While the few remaining passengers are battling with each other to take their chance in the river, Emmett is going in the opposite direction. Downwards, downwards, downwards, through a barricade of furniture and detritus. It catches his breath to see the lower deck is mostly underwater. He calls out, 'Abigail, where are you? It's me Emmett.'

His heart sinks. There is no reply. There is an explosion of light and then suddenly instant blackness as the bulkhead lights fail. For a moment he is disorientated. Then he pushes his way with difficulty against the icy-cold tidal wave of water now streaming in fast, all the time calling out her name. Is he wasting his time? Is he putting his own life at risk, when maybe she's been rescued already? Should he continue his search? Maybe she fell over when the boat hit the obstacle, and she's lying unconscious? Is it already too late? His heart is beating faster and faster until the sound of it in his ears is more consuming than the storm overhead, with its insistent thunder emphasising the trauma of the night.

Then he hears a faint cry. 'I'm in here. Help, help me please. Someone help me. I'm trapped.'

With renewed energy he pushes his way through the water, which is getting dangerously deeper all the time, his feet slipping and sliding as the boat lists further.

'Coming Abby, coming, hold on.'

'Emmett, is that you? I'm here, in the Ladies toilet.' She is holding her phone above her head, a dim light shining and reflecting on the water's surface.

'Yes, I can see you now. Save your breath, I'm coming to get you out.'

'Oh God Emmett, I'm so scared.' She tries to swivel around to look at him, but her foot is stuck tight. However, Emmett can only see that she is up to her waist in water.

He is at her side and she feels him grab at her. She cries out, 'Oh thank God Emmett, thank God, it's you. Can you get me out, my foot is stuck tight?'

Emmett dives beneath the water and yanks at her ankle and she cries out in pain.

He's back up for breath, 'Sorry.'

'Don't worry, don't worry, hurt me if you have to, I don't want to drown, Emmett, I don't want to die.'

'You're *not* going to die. Trust me.'

The water is slowly inching upwards, the cold setting into their bones, chilling them to the marrow. Abby is shivering. She tries to control her chattering teeth as she says, 'I'm so cold Emmett, I'm so very, very cold.' She's desperately trying to hold back the tears, then she blurts out, 'It's no good, you need to save yourself. Go, it doesn't matter. I'll be fine.'

He ignores her, takes a huge intake of breath and dives down again. He wriggles her foot and realises the only thing holding her tight is the strap of her handbag which has wrapped itself around her ankle.

He's back up. 'Can you try lifting your foot up as far as you can?'

'I'll try. Why, what's trapping me?'

'Your handbag strap.' He looks around, 'Try taking your weight with your hands, push up on the sink.' He mentally crosses his fingers hoping that the plumber was better than most and the sink will hold her weight.

With another intake of breath, he dives down, and with her heaving upwards as hard as she can and him wriggling the strap, pulling at her foot, twisting it this way and that, knowing that each move will be causing immense pain, she is free.

She flings her arms around him and hugs him, unable to control her sobs and gratitude. He can't help smiling, but disentangles her quickly. 'No time for that, we've got to get out of here somehow before it sinks completely.'

'How?'

By now the water is up to their shoulders. There is no light, just black.

'Hang onto me as tight as possible. We'll keep upright for as long as we can.'

With trembling voice, she asks, 'Then what?'

'What do you think?'

'Emmett, I know what you're saying, but I can't do it. I'm so claustrophobic, I've never even swum in the sea. I know what you're saying. I can't swim underwater, I can't.'

'No choice honey. Forget everything, concentrate on me being there to help you, I'll get you out somehow. I know what I'm doing, trust me.'

She thinks, *he keeps saying that.*

The water is coming in faster and faster and the ship is inclining even more, but Emmett pulls Abigail behind him, their faces upturned, almost touching the ceiling, breathing in the last air available, before suddenly the water is at ceiling height.

Abigail takes the deepest breath she can, fighting the panic building within her as she feels Emmett almost pulling her arms out of the sockets until, miraculously, they are on the surface of the water. He shouts, 'As fast as you can, swim away from the boat, it's going down and it's going to take us with it.'

She can feel the river current together with the pull of the boat just as Emmett said dragging her down as she wildly battles against the water, debris hitting her from all directions. As Abigail's head continually dips below the water, the sound of screams and sirens are muffled. There are flashing lights everywhere. A crushing feeling of tiredness is slowing her down. She wonders if this really how her life will end? Hannah. *Who will look after my Hannah?*

Out of nowhere there are hands pulling her up out of the water, dragging her into a boat.

'This one's OK, what about him over there?'

'Please find Emmett, you must find Emmett, he saved my life.' Tears mingle with river water. Then everything goes blank.

***

When Caroline sees Emmett and Abigail together, she forgets she is wanted by the law because she is consumed with jealousy. How dare Emmett use her former oldest friend to get at her? How dare Abigail now be part of Emmett's life? But before she can control her rage there is another problem, more imminent. The boat is floundering. Caroline's life is infinitely more important, in her view, than anyone else's. Immediately she pushes through the crowd, yelling and screaming at people to, '*Get out of my way! Move!*' until she finds a young man in uniform.

'Get me off this goddamn boat and fast, if you know what's good for you.'

Alan looks at this demanding creature, and says as temperately as his beating heart will allow, 'Madam, I'm trying to rescue everyone, if you can just stay calm—'

'Calm! We're sinking, how can I stay calm?' She grabs his sleeve. 'Where's the captain?'

Should Alan tell her? Explain how he wrestled with him to get control of the boat? How in the struggle for survival, Stuart Petersen smashed his head against the bulkhead, blood everywhere and then died? How Alan's first thought wasn't the passengers, but his wife and his unborn baby and how for a brief moment he grappled with his conscience as he considered saving himself before those now in his charge?

Then suddenly everyone is vying for his attention.

'Please you've got to get me off, my kid's alone at home.'

'I can't swim, you've got to get me on a lifeboat.'

'I can't find my girlfriend, have you seen her, she's wearing a pink dress?'

And bizarrely, 'I need to be at Scottie's, I'm not supposed to be here. I've got a show just after midnight.'

'Please folks, please.' For the previous five minutes Alan has been struggling to get the lifeboat mechanism to work. It's rusted through. In desperation he starts handing out lifejackets. 'Put these on, help is on its way, and please, please don't panic.'

'Should we jump overboard to save ourselves?'

'Yeah, should we?'

'He doesn't know, he's just a kid, where's the sodding captain?'

Further down the boat, Alan sees a man with great difficulty mounting a table. He hears him pleading for people to listen to him and stay calm. He sounds American. At least Alan thinks, someone is on his side. He is about to call out to him to join forces for the evacuation when Caroline grabs his arm. She has shoved an elderly woman out of the way, and sidled up to Alan, forcing tears into her eyes. 'I'm sorry I yelled at you. I was distraught. It's because my daughter's in labour. I need to be at her side.'

Her brain has computed that yelling and screaming at this twenty-something isn't going to work. She has to appeal to his better nature. Guile has to be her weapon. Strangely, she couldn't have said anything more powerful to Alan. Instantly he has connected with her. Especially when her next words are, 'What can I do to help?'

'Really? Here, help me dish these out.' He points to the pile of lifejackets lying on the floor.

The boat takes an unexpected list, and Caroline manages to fake a fall against Alan. 'Sorry, oh God, I think I'm going to pass out,' she says and then pretends to do so. Alan doesn't know what to do. He can't drop her on the ground, simply leave her lying there. Besides, everyone else is too busy saving themselves. There's nothing for it, he shoves a lifejacket on her and picks her up in his arms. By this time most people near to him are either scrabbling to climb down the side of the ship, or have already leaped into the water.

Caroline moans. Alan stares at her. Is she feigning pain? He can't decide. But who would do that when their life is at stake? She momentarily opens her eyes and whispers, 'Tell my daughter my last thoughts were of her and the baby. Ask her to call the baby after me, if it's a girl.' Then she slumps her head to the side again.

There's nothing for it. Alan feels obliged to rescue this obviously tormented woman. Although there is a fleeting moment of guilt when he thinks that maybe he should be the last one to leave the riverboat, bearing in mind he has now taken the role of Captain. At the back of his mind is a worry that there will be an enquiry into why he left the boat before all the passengers. He is in a dilemma. Should he abandon this lifeless creature? The boat is listing so badly now that the railing is not too far away from the surface of the river. He decides to gently lower Caroline into the water, all the time hoping the water will shock her awake. Seemingly it doesn't, and as her head turns into the water, he is terrified she will drown. He jumps in after her.

He can feel the drag of the boat and the tide straining against them as he pulls Caroline towards the shore. He hauls himself onto the slippery river bank, exhausted and turns towards her. Miraculously, suddenly, unexpectedly she is awake, sitting up, coughing and spluttering.

His voice hardly audible, he asks, 'Are you all right?'

She smiles back at him weakly. 'Yes, I'm fine. Thank you for saving me.'

'I need to go back,' he says, pointing at the boat, 'for the others. Will you be OK if I leave you here?'

'Of course, you go, I'll be OK here. Don't worry about me.'

He wades back into the water and proceeds to swim towards the boat, even though he can see rescue boats are coming. It doesn't matter, it's his job. Before he is half-way across the river he watches, horrified, as the boat upends and as if in slow motion, gently drops beneath the water line with a final whirlpool of water sucking the last remaining sections of the boat.

Then silence.

Moments later he is hauled onto a rescue boat. He sobs, 'I was trying to go back to save them. Oh God! I was trying to go back, you've got to believe me. I had to rescue the lady. The lady over there. She needs help.'

The two men look at one another and pull a face. 'Yeah, it's OK son. We believe you.'

The other man looks to where Alan is pointing.

There is no-one there.

Caroline has gone.

CHAPTER TWENTY-FIVE

Emmett is hovering around outside the hospital ward. He stops one of the nurses. 'I need to see one of your patients.'

'Visiting hours aren't for another half an hour, sorry.'

'Please ma'am, it's Abigail Davidson.'

The nurse stares at him. 'You're American, aren't you?'

'Yes ma'am, can you tell?'

'Obviously. I can hear your accent. I'm not stupid,' she replies tartly.

'Course not, I would never assume such a terrible thing.'

She peers at him suspiciously. 'Are you another reporter, because if you are—'

'No, I'm her—boyfriend.'

'Her boyfriend?'

'And I rescued her. You know from the boat.'

'Yes, I know all about that.'

Emmett watches as she screws her face up, her eyes narrowing and then says, 'All right, but you'd better tiptoe in, and if Sister catches you in there, it wasn't anything to do with me.'

He leans down and pecks the nurse on her cheek. 'You're a star.'

The nurse blushes and shoves him away, suddenly melting. 'Go on with you. Honestly, you Yanks are all alike.'

Abigail is sitting up in bed, her eyes shut as she gently dozes.

'Dreaming of me?' Emmett asks.

She opens her eyes at the sound of his voice. 'As if.' Her tears well up. 'Oh Emmett, thank you for saving me. If you hadn't been there—and Hannah, what would Hannah have done—and my mum would have been—'

'And I would have been pretty cut up too.'

'Would you, would you really?' she asks, her brow furrowing, her eyes misty.

'I can't tell you how sorry I am, the way all this turned out. I can't forgive myself. I shouldn't have gone along with the scam. I blame myself totally. I should have known better. All those poor people. I'll never ever forget or forgive myself.'

'How was it your fault? It was Caroline that organised the trip. Caroline chose the boat. And who was to know the captain was a drunk?'

'But I encouraged all you girls. None of you would have been there if I hadn't have wanted to nail Caroline, so it was all for nothing. Lives lost for nothing. Your friends could have been killed.'

Abigail asks tentatively, 'How many died? No-one will tell me.'

'Miraculously only five in the end. There was an elderly couple, a teenager, and the captain. And one missing person, presumed dead.'

'Caroline?'

He asks wryly, 'How did you know?'

The two of them are silent until Abigail asks, 'What happened exactly?'

Emmett drags his chair closer to Abigail. 'As far as I can tell the captain was told that very night it would be his and the boat's last river trip. Well, everyone got *that* bit right. So, the story goes, Alan Fraser, his deputy, found him drunk as a lord in the wheelhouse. He wrestled with him to take control and that's when it hit the barge. You know the rest.'

'What happened to this Alan Fraser?'

Emmett takes a deep breath. 'This is where I believe him, and the authorities don't. He reckons that an attractive blonde woman fainted in his arms and he felt obliged to save her from drowning. He alleges he left her on the riverbank and then was going back to the boat when he realised it was too late as it sank before his eyes.'

'Bloody hell.'

Then both of them say in one breath, 'Caroline.'

'Yup, that's what I think too. I've tried my best to help persuade them his story rings true, but you know what the authorities are like. They love to blame the person in charge, or not in charge as the case may be. Although there is a glimmer of hope. They've rescued the CCTV system from the wreck and are trying to salvage information from it. Hopefully that will exonerate him.'

'But Caroline? I thought there was such a thing as Karma?'

'There is, but sometimes you have to wait a long time for it.'

'How long?'

'Who knows? Tomorrow? Next year? Just before she meets her Maker?'

'Sometimes, no more than sometimes, a lot more than sometimes I think life is pretty unfair. I mean, that poor man Alan.'

Emmett smiles. 'Not totally poor, there was an upside, he ended up in the same hospital as his wife while she was giving birth to his baby, so he did get to see it being born. He's an honest guy. He admitted to the authorities that he'd been in two minds to go to the hospital when he got the call his wife was in labour, but felt duty-bound to stay.'

'Crikey, so it could all have been worse?'

'Worse or better. He says that maybe if he and the captain hadn't fought over his drinking, it's possible they wouldn't have hit the barge.'

Abigail looks horrified. 'That's some guilt he has to carry around with him. On the other hand, wouldn't the captain, if he was that drunk, have hit the barge anyway?'

Emmett rubs his chin and ponders, 'We will never know.'

'Such is life, eh? What did his wife have anyway?'

Emmett looks at her in amazement. 'A boat has sunk; there's been untold trauma on the river; inquiries have begun; questions have been asked in your House of Commons; people have died; and the woman asks what was it, boy or girl? How the hell should I know?'

Abigail laughs. 'You're hopeless.'

'Wanna hear more irony? The conglomerate, who were taking over the cruise line, have backed out because of the bad publicity.'

A bell sounds, and Emmett looks around. 'Do I have to go now?'

'No, silly, this is the time when you were supposed to come in.'

A motley group of people make their way into the ward clutching grapes, newspapers and all manner of things that folk bring in to clutter hospital wards much to the annoyance of the domestic staff and nurses.

'Seems like I do most of my talking to you when you're in bed,' Emmett jokes.

'I beg your pardon? Not so loud please. People might get the wrong idea.'

He leans forward even more and whispers, 'I'd *love* to get the wrong idea with you, any chance? Especially considering Caroline has accused us of being bed-buddies to all your friends. I'd hate to disappoint them.'

Abigail taps his hand. 'Don't be so naughty.' But she's beaming. 'Thought you were headed back to the States, or are you still on the hunt for Caroline?'

'No, and no.'

'What?'

'No, I'm not headed back for the States, and as far as Caroline is concerned, I don't want to know.'

'I don't get it?' And then Abigail's mouth does a round and almost silent, 'O'.

'Yup, got the sack. Been *let go*. Let the firm down. Cost them *far* too much money. Whatever. That woman's trouble. Let her be someone else's problem and not mine.'

Her heart is beating so loudly she's worried Emmett might hear. She tentatively asks him, 'So how long are you here for?'

'Until I find employment, which I might add is almost imminent.'

'You're kidding?'

He raises his eyebrows. 'Do I look like a kidder?' Then he frowns. 'Don't answer that. I don't want to know. You may, or may not, depending on whether Mr Smithers agrees with Mrs Smithers, be looking at their new security consultant at Smithers, Smithers and Smithers Jnr.'

'That's an awful lot of Smithers.'

'It sure is.'

CHAPTER TWENTY-SIX

Five months later

It's Sunday morning, the sky is a cold blue, without a cloud. The air hangs, freezing the very back of one's throat with its iciness. The hoar frost is clinging to the trees with its spiky decoration. There is silence everywhere. That is until Emmett bangs his boots hard on the mat outside the back door, shaking off the snow. As he opens it, Abigail shouts from upstairs, 'Coffee's on the stove, down in two ticks.'

He leans down and takes the lead off the mongrel who is leaning on his legs, panting.

'That was some walk, wasn't it Smithers?'

Abigail grabs Emmett from behind and hugs him. 'Missed you.'

'I've only been gone for an hour, what are you like? Where's little Hannah?'

'Emmett, stop calling her little Hannah. She's taller than me and I really think you should think up another name for that stray mongrel. If your boss finds out you've called it after him, you can kiss goodbye to your promotion.'

Emmett pulls Abigail into him and hugs her, his hand amorously roaming over her body. 'Emmett, no. What if Hannah comes down and catches us?'

His voice thick with emotion, he asks, 'What if she does? We share the same bedroom. What do you think she reckons we do in there, play Scrabble?'

They sit down, and Emmett zaps the remote and turns on the television.

'Oh, not the News channel *again*, Emmett. Can't we have a break from—oh my God, oh my God, look!' Abigail stands up and frantically points at the television. 'Turn it up! Quick! Turn it up, I can't hear what they're saying.'

'…immigrants who landed in Dover at 3am this morning. Suspicions were raised when it was clear that none of the immigrants appear to have known the blonde female who had been rescued with them. At the usual border force checkpoint, it was discovered that the female was none other than Caroline Smith, who is wanted in connection with various Ponzi schemes around the planet. Caroline Smith, aka Caroline Armitage, aka Caroline Trent, is now in police custody. It is unlikely she will be given bail.

'On a lighter note, a pensioner who had been buying tickets for the lottery for over sixty years has scooped the jackpot of over sixty-eight million pounds. Mrs Wilkins, 75, of…'

'What about that!' Abigail screams. 'Who'd have thought it?'

'Yeah, told you we should keep doing your UK lottery. Sixty-eight mil! Wow! That's some haul.'

Emmett ducks as Abigail hurls a tea towel at him. 'Schmuck,' she hollers.

'Told you Karma would get her in the end.'

Abigail nods, 'You were right.'

Emmett continues puzzling over the daily crossword, head down, while Abigail suddenly wonders, is he really pleased Caroline's been caught? She can't tell from his poker-face. Is there a little piece of him that wishes she was still on the run? After all Emmett had admitted to Abigail that he'd slept with her, surely that hadn't been just a *duty*? In fact, not a *duty* at all considering it was the main reason he'd got the sack. His boss took a dim view of such goings on. At that time, she'd panicked a little, imagining him and Caroline together, worried that it was all happening again, Caroline sleeping with her boyfriend before she'd slept with him. Would that conniving bitch wriggle out of her arrest and hunt them down so that she could ruin yet another of Abigail's relationships? She looks at Emmett and compares him to Baz. Maybe not this time she considers. Surely Karma has kicked in, hasn't it?

What was Karma anyway, if not a watered-down version of Justice? How about the people who died on the boat that fateful night? How about all the hundreds of people hurt by Caroline and her scams all over the planet, the ones who'd lost their houses, families, lives even? Was the fact Caroline would be banged up in prison for a few years and then be let out on parole, having served less than the term first decided, was that a good enough Karma for them?

A sudden memory would flash into her mind unexpectedly at odd times with a dreadful feeling of sadness that would overcome her as she thought of the fun the two girls had enjoyed as little kids and then teenagers. There was no Karma in the world that could make up for the fact her friend had turned into her enemy. And what was it all for? What reason? What had she done wrong? How had she brought that upon herself?

Abigail studies Emmett quietly sitting there, perched on the kitchen stool, draining the dregs of his coffee mug, and wonders if she can erase all the bad memories and start afresh with this man, the man who saved her life at risk of his own. Is he starting afresh with her, doing a job he tolerates, living with a teenager with no bloodline involvement, and a woman approaching middle-age? Is that going to be enough for him? Make him happy so that he will stay with her *for as long as they both shall live?*

Will they make it work, or will it be another reason to hope for Karma to hit when it all goes wrong?

Emmett suddenly looks up and realises Abigail is staring at him. His face creases into a smile, his eyes crinkling, 'Any chance of another cup of coffee?'

She smiles back, 'Why not? Why ever not?'

OTHER BOOKS BY THIS AUTHOR:

TIZER, COMICS AND CRISPS

INSPECTOR ORANGE IN THE
UNDERBUILD WITH A BLUNT SPOON

THE FRYING PAN IN THE NIGHT
(FEATURING THE AWFUL
INSPECTOR ORANGE)

THE COPY THIEF
(FEATURING THE ANNOYING
INSPECTOR ORANGE)

DON'T MIX THE DEAD

THE SOAPSTAR MURDERS

PICKING OFF THE PETALS

TROUBLE ON DORSET DRIVE

SOMETHING VERY NASTY
IN MY BOOT!

FIFTEEN MINUTES OF SHAME

JUST A WINK AND A SMILE

LONDON TO MILAN

A STAB IN THE BACK

UNEXPECTED ITEM IN THE

HUSBAND'S LUGGAGE

THE SHORE